I0582073

FABRICATED love

KATRINA MARIE

Nobody deserves the dedication to this book like Casa Cavasos. It's one of my fave restaurants, and there's no way this book would have been finished without them. Thank you for always taking care of me, when I sit in that booth to write.

prologue

MY PHONE VIBRATES in my pocket. Pulling it out, I take a quick glance at the screen. My brother's face flashes across it. Nope. I'm not doing this right now. I watch as it rolls over to voicemail. Seconds later, a text flashes across my screen.

PIERCE

Where are you? You're supposed to be at this business dinner.

My fingers hover over the text area to reply. How do I tell him I don't want a part in the family business? I mean, I've told everyone repeatedly, but they keep trying to reel me back in. For whatever reason, they can't take no for an answer.

This isn't worth my time right now. I told them I wasn't going to be at the dinner. I have plans. Do those plans involve me hanging at the local bar? Absolutely. But I don't owe an explanation to anyone.

A body knocks into me from the back and my phone flies out of my hand onto the crowded floor. Damn it. This isn't what I need right now. I move forward to grab it before someone steps on it. As much as I love working at Whoopsie Daisy, I don't get paid enough to buy a new phone if this one breaks.

Somebody gets to it before I do. Maybe I should wait to see what they are going to do. They'll either be an awesome human and find who it belongs to. Or they'll pocket it and hope they can get it unlocked.

A guy with shaggy brown hair steps in front of me, holding out my phone. "I think this may be yours."

"How did you know?" I reach out to grab it, and our fingers touch for the briefest moment. A jolt of electricity runs through me. That's never happened before.

He shrugs and pushes his hair away from his face. "I may have been the one who knocked it out of your hand."

"Well, thanks for being a standup person." I laugh to let him know I'm joking. "Can I, uh, buy you a drink?"

Never in my life have I been nervous talking to guys. What makes this one so different?

"Sure. I have a bit before I have to help clear off the stage."

"Whoa, hold up." I wave my hands between us. "Are you a part of Crooked Halo?"

The band plays here frequently since they are good friends with someone involved with Out of the Ashes, but I've never seen this man when they've played before. Maybe he's new.

"Kind of." He tilts his head to the side, like he's confused with his own answer. "I work with the crew. We basically set things up and take them down for the band. I've been with them for a few years now."

"Why is this the first time I'm seeing you?" I point at him as if there's another person talking to me. "I've been here almost every time the band has played."

He shrugs his shoulders. "What can I say? It's one of the mysteries of being a part of the crew. We're only seen when we want to be."

"You act like you're some kind of magician."

Another shrug. "I can thank all my years in theatre. If I wasn't on stage, I was in the tech crew, and we did a lot behind the scenes."

"Interesting." Theatre was never my thing in high school. "And why did you want to be seen tonight?"

"I wasn't trying to be." He runs a hand through his hair. "Bumping into you wasn't part of the plan."

"Well, I'm glad you did." I turn toward the bar and nod for him to follow. He said he had a bit of time after all.

"Hey, what can I get for ya?" Eric, one of my favorite bartenders, asks.

"Can I get a salty dog?" I glance over at the man beside me. "What will you have?"

"Beer is fine. You know my usual."

Eric nods and gets to work making our drinks.

"Well, I guess you really do come with the band if Eric knows your order."

"I wasn't lying." He shakes his head. "By the way, what's your name?"

Holy crap, I forgot about not getting names. "Paula. You?"

"Tristan. It's nice to meet you."

He moves closer to me as Eric slides our drinks across the bar. I can't remember the last time I felt so at ease talking to someone. I mean, I'm friendly with the girls at work, but this is different. Someone I might be interested in if I did relationships.

"So, how long are you in town?" I take a sip of my drink. Just because he comes and goes doesn't mean we can't have a little fun.

"A couple of days, I think." He tilts his head to the side as if that will help him come to the right conclusion. "I know the band was going to work on a project with Devin, but I'm not sure how long they plan on sticking around."

"Do you have to be wherever they are?"

"Actually, no." He moves his forearm to the edge of the bar and leans on it. "We usually get leave time when they are working on stuff because they aren't' doing any shows. I usually go home, but I could hang around here for a little longer."

It's good to know I'm not the only one feeling the chemistry. Though, I don't know how I feel about the couple of days part. That feels a little too long for what I'm comfortable with.

"How about we start with one night?" Too forward? Maybe. But it beats talking to my family, and he's cute.

He rears his head back, surprised by my suggestion. I'm guessing most people he's seen don't usually come right out with their intentions.

"Um, yeah. That works, too." His cheeks are bright red, and I don't think I've ever made a man blush.

"Let's finish our drinks, then get out of here."

He doesn't argue, but the smile crossing his face lets me know he's not opposed to the idea.

"Wow, you live way out here, don't you?" He's standing with me on the front porch as I unlock my door.

"Yeah. It gives me the privacy I want and I'm away from my family. It's a double win." I shrug and push the door open.

"I take it you're not close to your family." He follows me inside and shuts the door behind him. "Any chance I get, I go home to see my family."

Shaking my head, I laugh. "You don't have the family I do. They feel the need to butt in on every aspect of my life."

I really don't want to get into this with him. It's too heavy a subject and I don't know that he needs all of this information. Especially for one night. He may be coming in with bigger expectations, but I can't promise him that.

Honestly, we should have gotten a hotel instead of coming to my house. It's like I'm incapable of making a good decision. Well, that's not entirely true. Discussing my family just makes me moody.

"That's actually understandable. I think we all have those people in our lives who think they know what's best for us."

With those few words my bad mood has gone just as quickly as it arrived. I'm glad he's not judging me. I get enough of that from everyone else.

I'm only hoping we can keep this up for the rest of the night because I don't want this to be another mistake.

"Thanks for not pressing too much."

"Hey." He holds his hands up. "We're hanging out for fun. Not to bring family drama into things. No offense, but that feels a bit much for a first date."

I can't help the laugh that falls from my lips. "This is what you consider a first date? Most guys would definitely classify this as a hook up."

He holds his hands up in the air. "Nobody said you were getting any of this just because I came home with you."

"What other reason did you think we were leaving?" He is different than most guys I've ever met, even briefly. Or maybe I misread his smile? I mean, he did blush when we were at the bar.

"I know exactly what you were insinuating, but I'm not that kind of guy. I never have been." He takes a few steps back toward the door. "We can hang out and get to know each other a little bit. Or, I can go back to my hotel room."

"Wait, you have a hotel?" God, this information would have been good to know before we left the bar.

Then he wouldn't know where I live, and this wouldn't become an issue later on. As cute as I think he is, I don't know if I can just hang out with him. It's not something I'm used to doing.

"Yes." He draws out. "Why is that important?"

"Because we could have gone there instead of here." The words should have to be said. Hook ups are always better when you don't bring them home.

"I would have said the same thing there." He shakes his head as if he's disappointed in me. Who knows, maybe he is. "You know what? This may be a bad idea."

"No." I hold my hands out as if that can stop him from walking out the door. "It's not a bad idea. We can hang out."

He's trying to be the good guy here, and I'm not making it easy. My head is telling me to let him walk out the door. We clearly aren't here for the same reasons. But my gut...that's saying something else entirely. There's a possibility not being intimate may be a good thing.

"Are you sure?"

I don't blame him for questioning me. I would if I were in his shoes. The only solution is to push through the awkwardness I've created.

"Yep. What do people do when they just hang out?"

"You're kidding, right?"

Wow, I feel like a complete dumbass. Clearly, I've been single way too long. Or, I've had a bit too much fun. I don't normally stick around when I meet up with guys.

"Uh, no." I shrug and move toward the living room,

hoping he'll follow instead of run out the door. "I don't have a ton of experience in just hanging out."

At least, not since high school. But I'm not telling him that. There's no way I'm going to look good if I give further explanation.

"Oh, well, we can watch TV, talk, or play card games if you have any cards."

"Absolutely no board, or card, games." I shake my head. It's one of my worst nightmares from my childhood with my overly competitive siblings. I never had a good time, and they did their best to make me feel dumb. And they wonder why I don't want anything to do with them, or the winery.

"I'm sensing some trauma."

"You have no idea."

"Okay, so games are out." He studies me for a second. "We can just watch a movie. Unless you have any video games."

"Actually." I grin. "I do have a gaming console. It's probably my favorite racing game ever."

"That sounds like a challenge."

"Bring it on, buddy. I'm about to demolish you."

"If you say so." He moves to sit on the sofa. "Do you need help with anything?"

"Not really. It's literally just pushing a few buttons." I move toward the console and turn it on at the same time I turn on the TV. "There should be beer and water in the fridge if you're thirsty."

"Water sounds good."

I hear a pillow hit the coffee table when he stands up.

At least he's comfortable enough in his own skin to rummage through my fridge while I'm getting the game going.

Now that the startup menu is on the screen, I grab the controllers and move to the sofa. MC comes back at the same time with two bottles of water in his hand. I mean, a beer sounds nice to calm my nerves, but hydration is probably more important. I still have to work tomorrow, and I refuse to show up to Whoopsie Daisy hungover. Not when I'm hoping to become closer to the ladies I work with.

"Are you ready to get beat?" He grins over at me as I hand him a controller.

"In your dreams."

This is the weirdest one night stand I've ever had. Despite how easily we seem to get along, there's no way I'm continuing this past tonight. Especially not when he's out of town so often and doesn't even live here. A night of racing will have to do.

CHAPTER ONE

"WELCOME TO WHOOPSIE DAISY, what can I help you with?" My voice is almost like a tune as the bell above the door rings. I don't even bother looking up before the words are out of my mouth.

"Hey Sister."

My head snaps up at the sound of my baby brother's voice. "Parker, what are you doing here?"

"What? I can't come see what my favorite sibling is up to?"

"You better watch out. The other siblings may get jealous." I laugh. "Now, why are you really here?"

His strides are long as he makes his way to the counter. "This is pretty much the only time I'm able to see you. It's not like you come around."

I watch him as he studies the various arrangements under the glass counter. It's not anything that's real, just examples of some of the things we can do. Well, not me. I don't' have a creative bone in my body. The only reason I applied to work here is because I liked the vibe of everyone here.

"There's a reason I don't come around often."

"Yeah, yeah, I know." He waves away my comment. "But...you know you'll need to talk to Mom and Dad at some point."

"It's not them I have an issue speaking with." Well, that's not completely true. My Dad is pretty high up there with folks I don't want to converse with. But he's not the one constantly putting pressure on me to do something I don't want to do.

"You'll have to talk to Pierce. There's no avoiding it."

"I've been doing a good job of it for the past six months." I shrug my shoulder. "As far as I'm concerned it can last a lot longer."

"Oh my God. The two of you are like children."

"We're someone's children, so it's appropriate."

"Not really. But I'm not getting between the two of you. Us younger siblings shouldn't have to play referee."

Do I feel bad that it happens sometimes? Yes, I do. It's not their job to run interference, but Pierce can't seem to be an adult about anything when it comes to the family business. He's the oldest. It's his responsibility. I don't know why I have to be a part of it. Besides, there are six of us total. Why can't five handle the business? The only thing I've ever wanted is to live my life.

"I'm sorry. I promise I won't put you in the middle of any arguments I have with my brother."

"You aren't the only one that does it," Parker sighs. "But...you won't like what I have to say next."

"Why?"

He turns back toward the front of the shop. No doubt making sure we aren't about to have any customers. If he's doing that, it means I'm about to be pissed.

"Because it's time for the family vacation."

"No way. We just went on one." At least, it feels like we did. I realize the date, and nope we haven't had our yearly stress filled vacation.

"Well, it's time again. Mom, Dad, and Pierce want you there."

He still won't look at me. Not that I blame him. I will never understand why my parents make these things mandatory.

"It's not like I have a choice." I get they want the family together at the same time, but what are they going to do when the rest of my siblings get into relationships and start having families. There's no way their partners will want to go on these trips. Although, I guess in their eyes it's a future problem.

"True." He nods. "It's not as bad as you make it out to be, though."

Maybe for them. I've always been the black sheep of the family. Being with all my siblings at one time is fun until we get into a disagreement or whip out the board games. That's when everything goes downhill.

"When is this marvelous weekend of family bonding supposed to happen? I'll need to see if I can take off." Plus side, it's the beginning of wedding season, which means I'll be needed to help out.

"Take off for what?" Emily asks as she comes into the

room. She's carrying a few bouquets in her hands and almost drops one.

My brother rushes to her rescue. "Here, let me help you." He gives her the smile I've seen him give dozens of girls when we drink together.

"Oh, thank you." Emily says, unfazed by my brother's charisma.

"No problem." He holds two of the bouquets as she sets the ones in her arms on the shelf beside the counter. After he hands her the ones he's holding, he leans on the counter. "So, who do I have the pleasure of meeting?"

"Knock it off, Parker. She's taken."

Emily's eyes widen as she realizes he was trying to give her some tired pickup line. "Yeah, I'm happily taken, but I'm Emily." She holds her hand out. "And you are?"

My brother side eyes me as he shakes her hand. "Parker. I'm Paula's baby brother."

"Oh, how nice to meet you." I don't miss the curious glance she shoots my way. I haven't really talked much about my family. Mostly because they drive me up the wall, but I try really hard to keep my personal life away from work.

"He was just leaving." I make my way from behind the counter and push him toward the door.

"Actually, can I buy one of these bouquets?"

Rolling my eyes, I let go of him. "Which girl of the week are you giving it to now?"

"I would never." He holds his hand to his chest as if he's surprised. "They are for Mom."

"You're such a suck up." I wait for him to grab a bouquet, then stomp back to the register to ring him up.

"And that's why I'm the favorite." He grins at me as he hands me his card.

"Oh, is that what Mom tells you? I'm almost certain she says that to all of us." I notice Emily doing her best not to listen in on our conversation. She's not subtle about it.

"It's true for me, though." He takes his card back and shoves it in his pocket. "I'll text you the information. Love you, Sis."

"Love you, too." I watch him leave the shop to make sure he's not going to add anything else.

"So that's your brother?" Emily laughs. "He seems like a handful."

"He's probably the one who causes the most trouble out of all of us."

Emily scrunches her eyebrows together. "All of you? How many siblings do you have?"

It's times like these I remember she's an only child. But I'm certain her struggle has been the same as mine with the need to live up to parental expectations.

"There are six of us. I'm the second oldest." I wonder if she can hear the irritation in my voice. Parker's right. It's not like everything has always been horrible. I just hate the way I'm expected to do every little thing they want instead of living my own life.

"I can't even imagine the chaos that is when your whole family is together." The look of sheer horror on her face is comical. "What is happening that you'll need time off for? Is everything okay?"

Of course, she goes straight to worrying about me and my family. It's kind of her role in all the friendships here. She's the one who looks after everyone's emotional well-being.

"Everything is fine." I assure her. "My family does a big vacation every year. I didn't realize we haven't done one this year until my brother reminded me."

"Do you know the dates?"

"Not yet." I shrug my shoulders and wipe down the counter. It's not dirty, but it does give me something to do. "My brother is sending me the information. If I can't take off, it's not a huge deal. There will be another one next year."

If I miraculously get out of this one, it means I'll be able to put off the uncomfortable conversations my dad and Pierce want to have. I still don't understand why I'm needed when they have my older brother.

Emily leans on the counter thinking for a moment. "I'm sure it won't be a problem. As long as it's not in the middle of a wedding cluster, we'll be fine without you."

Damn. That's not what I wanted her to say at all. Maybe I should have been more open about myself when I first started working here. I guess this is what I get for being more of a recluse instead of being outgoing and letting them in.

"Cool. I'll find out the dates as soon as possible."

"Let me ask you a question." Emily bumps my shoulder. "Do you even want to go on this family vacation?

Because your body language says you'd rather walk across hot coals a thousand times over."

"Let's just say it's not my favorite thing in the world to do. But it's one of the many expectations I have placed on me, and sadly...there's no way out of it."

She snorts and I don't think I've ever heard her make that sound.

"I know a thing or two about ridiculous expectations from parents. Sometimes it's best to be honest about them and let them know how you feel." She sighs and stands before turning toward the hallway. "But don't wait too long. I didn't learn that lesson until this year, and I'm kicking myself for not realizing what my parents were doing sooner. Like in my teen years."

With those parting words, she disappears down the dimly lit hallway. You'd think that's something her boyfriend would have fixed when renovating the back of the store. Though I can see why he didn't. It allows the space to be open but not completely visible.

Emily's advice bounces around in my head. While I love the idea of telling my parents to drop any and all expectations of me, they aren't the only one's who'd need to hear the words. My brothers and sister would have to be told as well. At this point it's easier to go and put on a fake smile than it is to get into a heated battle with them.

The bell above the door jingles as someone pushes open the door. I force a smile even though I'm feeling anything but happy at the moment. Fake it 'til you make it. The mantra I repeated to myself since I was a teen and had the silly idea my parents wouldn't want me to take part in the business.

It's funny how wrong I was all those years ago. Even still, they never give up. Maybe I can appeal to my brother during this trip. Surely, he's tired of staying on my ass about it.

Best not to worry about it right this second. I have time. For now, I'll worry about the customer who walked in.

tristan

"TRISTAN!" Dale pushes through the crowd at Out of the Ashes to get to me. The door is feet in front of me. I almost made it out with someone requesting something from me.

It's not that I dislike my job. I have a blast, but sometimes it feels like they are constantly looking at me to be their gopher.

The urge to keep walking and act like I didn't hear him is strong. It's not who I am, though. I would feel horrible, and I don't want to put myself through that.

Turning, I wait for him to catch up. "What's up?"

Hopefully I don't sound annoyed. If I do, it doesn't register to him because he's catching his breath and holds up a finger.

My foot taps despite trying to keep my cool. I just want to get back to the hotel. Though, it might be time to invest in a property here since we're in town so much. I'll get around to looking once I'm done doing whatever Dale needs.

Now that he's caught his breath he glances up and down. "Are you leaving already?"

"Yeah, I want to unwind since we just came off tour again."

"I totally get it. It's the whole reason we're building a studio out here. Being treated like a normal person in a town is nice, and it'll give us a place to hang out when we have down time."

He's not wrong. They've come here so often, they are practically locals. The people here don't get start struck anymore. Is this seriously what he wanted to talk to me about?

"I'll be checking out rental properties soon, or invest in a property soon."

"That's a good idea. This is our home away from home." He runs a hand through his hair. "Anyway, if you aren't busy, I have a favor to ask you."

So much for my day off. I've been with the band for a few years now, and I can't help but wonder how they got things done before I came along. They didn't have a crew when they started out.

"What do you need?"

There's no point in trying to deflect. Dale will give me the puppy dog eyes and knows I'll fold. One of these days I won't be such a pushover. There's only one night I stood my ground, and I regret not being my normal self in that one instance.

"So, you know Valentine's Day is coming up, right?"

"I'm aware."

"Well, me and some of the guys need to get some flowers ordered for our partners. But we want it to be a surprise so we can't use our personal cards."

Honestly, I'm shocked they all have joint accounts. I'm not sure how normal that is in celebrity relationships, but it seems odd they don't have at least one account of their own.

"Okay." I drawl. "Why do you need me?"

"Well, we know you talked to one of the women who runs the flower shop. We thought you might be able to get us a last-minute order and also put it on your card. You can expense it, of course."

Do I want to do this? Absolutely not. At least he doesn't want me to get lingerie or anything. That would be embarrassing.

"Is there any particular kind of flower you want me to make sure is included?"

He shrugs his shoulders. "I actually don't know. Let's say whatever they have that's not overdone."

As if that narrows it down. "Sure thing." I turn toward the door once again and pause. "Wait, are these for a special occasion outside of Valentine's Day?"

His cheeks turn a bright red before he nods. "That's one of the reasons it needs to be kept quiet without tracing it back to me. The other guys, they have no clue what to get their girlfriends."

I feel a lot better getting his now, but I hope he has

other stuff planned because I don't think an extravagant bouquet will be enough. Knowing him he probably has something up his sleeve. Honestly, I'm surprised they aren't already engaged. They've been together for years.

"Do you want me to send pictures of what they have available?"

"Absolutely not. What if she sees it over my shoulder or something? I trust your judgement."

Nodding, I turn toward the door. "I'll add it to my expense report." I call over my shoulder.

At this point, though, I should probably have a credit card to use for Crooked Halo expenditures. The number of times I've had to run to the store and get things for them before a show is ridiculous. Or, they could let me double check their stuff before we head to the venues.

"You're a lifesaver, Tristan." The door slams shut behind me. Hopefully he didn't have anything else to add to that statement. Maybe something like, you deserve a raise. I'm just happy we'll have some downtime for a bit.

The cold air bites through my t-shirt and I pull my jacket closed to zip it up. Winter in Texas isn't my favorite thing. It can be warm or freezing. Right now, it's a bit in the middle of the two.

My car is on the far end of the lot and I reach my hand into my pocket to unlock it. One of these days I need to invest in a vehicle that will auto start. Going from the cold outside to the cold inside isn't it for me.

As soon as I slide onto the driver seat, I turn on the car and put the heater on full blast. While the car warms up, I grab my phone out of my pocket to see what time

Whoopsie Daisy closes. I'd like to get this done today. Tomorrow, I'll check to see what places are available for rent in the area.

Staying in a rental with the band is cool at times, but I need my own space. Sometimes being in my room isn't enough. Staring at the same four walls day after day is monotonous.

The drive to the flower shop doesn't take long. That proves to be the same for anywhere you want to go in town. It's so small the drive to any store takes about fifteen max. That's if there's a small amount of traffic, which includes tractors. Never thought I'd say that.

A part of me hopes Paula is working in the front, but after the wedding we both attended, I'm terrified. Realistically, I could go to a flower shop in another town, or order online. But Dale is particular about using this one because he likes to keep things as local as possible.

You can do this. Deep breath in and out. Everything will be fine. Don't make it awkward when it doesn't have to be. Who am I kidding? There's a reason I never auditioned to be the lead in my high school theatre productions. Awkward is the only thing I put off. Especially when it comes to Paula.

Opening my car door, I glance around the parking spaces in front of the building. Her car is nowhere in sight. Maybe the Gods are smiling down on me today.

I close the door behind me and head to the shop. The bell above the door lets out a little jingle, but nobody says anything. I take another step into the shop and I hear her voice.

"Welcome to Whoopsie Daisy, how can I help you?"

The smile that accompanied her previous question dies as soon as she sees me.

"I, uh, need to order some flowers." I wave before shoving my hand in my pocket.

"Are you sure about that?"

"Yes." I nod. "For Valentine's Day."

A pained expression takes over her face, before slipping back to neutrality. "You realize we cut off taking orders yesterday, right? Except for the most basic bouquets we keep on hand."

Does the bite in her tone mean she's jealous? Hope that she actually feels something for me blossoms. I'm not here for her, though. It's strictly band business.

"Can you make an exception? Dale is proposing to his girlfriend and wants flowers to match the occasion."

"Why isn't he here ordering them if it's so important?"

Seriously, it's like she has to turn everything into an argument. It's been months since I've seen her. A warm fuzzy welcoming isn't something I expected, but the almost outright hostility is kind of annoying. Though, I'm pretty sure she's using it as a way to hide her emotions.

"Because he wants it to be a surprise."

"I don't feel like that's a valid excuse." She taps her fingers on the glass case.

"Please, Paula. They have a joint account and he doesn't want her to see the purchase. He wants it to be a total surprise for his proposal."

Her body loses some of the tension it held. "Oh, that's so sweet."

"Yes, it is, which is why I really need to get an order in for them."

She picks up a tablet and taps the screen before scrolling. This seems like a weird time to be looking at that instead of getting my order on the books.

"I'm sorry, I don't see where we would be able to fit it in. There's a reason the shop has a cutoff date. Especially with special orders where we'd need to get flowers we don't normally carry."

A small part of me feels like she's doing this on purpose. There has to be something she can do. Maybe I should have ordered from one of the bigger shops and just told Dale that I got them from here.

Who am I kidding? There's no way I would do that. I'm not sure why I even considered it. The blame could be laid at his feet for not giving me this task sooner. As much as he likes to plan these big gestures, he always rushes around last minute to bring them to fruition. Well, I usually have to do the rushing, but that's beside the point.

"Are you sure there's no way you can squeeze it in? It's just one teensy tiny order."

"Is it, though?" She tilts her head to the side, studying me.

"You're right." I sigh. "I guess I need to find another shop." My shoulders drop and I turn toward the door.

"Wait!" she calls out, and I stop in my tracks. "Let me ask my bosses if there's anything they can do."

"Thank you." I'm seconds from throwing my fist in the air in victory. But I don't want to celebrate too soon.

She disappears down the hallway behind the glass cases. I take a moment to study some of the smaller arrangements. I'm guessing they keep these out here for soon to be brides so they can have an idea for what they want. There are bouquets sitting on shelves on the wall. It's not cluttered though. They give each arrangement space to shine.

Paula rushes back into the room with a devious grin. I'm already wondering if I'm going to like whatever she has to say. I hope like hell it doesn't up the cost to squeeze in the order.

"Good news." She leans on the counter waiting for me to come closer. "They can fulfill the order for Dale. The other bouquets will be pretty generic, but they've decided to make an exception for you."

A sigh of relief escapes me. "That's gr—"

"But there's a caveat."

"How much is it going to cost?"

"Not money, but time." She's still smiling, but I know she has something up her sleeve.

"What do you mean?"

"My family goes on a yearly vacation, but I don't want to go alone. It makes it easier for them to pounce on me at the same time."

"Okay." I scratch my head. "I fail to see what that has to do with me."

"Well, you have a background in theatre, and we get along well enough."

"And?"

"I want you to go with me as my boyfriend. It's the only way they'll allow me to bring someone."

My mouth drops open. There's no way she thinks this is an even trade.

CHAPTER THREE

THE SHOCK on Tristan's face isn't something I factored into this plan. He tried talking to me at the wedding, even after I blew him off for months. I figured this would be a dream for him.

"So, do we have a deal?"

"I-I don't know." He shakes his head and stares at the ground. "Why would you even make that suggestion?"

To his credit, it is a half-cocked plan. It sparked after Kate said we could take the order. He doesn't need to know they didn't co-sign on it.

"You need something, I need something. It works for both of us." I only hope he doesn't hear the desperation in my voice. I cannot face my entire family on my own. They will come at me like starving lions.

Finally, he lifts his eyes until they meet mine, and there's fire in them. "Is this coming from you? Or did the bosses say it?"

Damn it. So much for trying to throw that in there.

"It's from me, okay." I pick at my nails while avoiding in and all eye contact with him. "They said they can fill your order. Even the ones for the other bandmates."

Tristan crosses his arms over his chest and smirks. "That's great. Can I give you the info and give you, my card?"

"Yeah." I grumble.

He moves closer and leans on the glass case. "You know, you didn't have to try to trick me into going on this trip with you."

"Okay." I roll my eyes. "How else would I have gotten you to agree to this?"

"By asking." He shakes his head as if it was the obvious answer. For him, maybe. But I don't typically ask for help. Anytime I've done it before it's come with strings attached.

"Sure, like you would have said yes after I basically gave you the cold shoulder at the wedding. Besides, I didn't even know you were back in town."

"Then why offer this now?"

"Because you were here. It's not like we dislike each other. We just want different things. And you are a safe option."

"But you know how much I travel." I can feel his eyes staring a hole into me. "How do you even know I'll be able to make the dates? It would have all been for nothing."

He has a point. I didn't even consider that. Especially when I don't know the dates for the vacation yet.

"Look." I sigh. "It wasn't a well thought out plan. I

know that, but I cannot be around my family for that long alone. It was worth throwing the idea out there."

"When is the trip?"

"I have no idea. My baby brother is supposed to send me the dates today."

His eyebrows scrunch in confusion. "Wait, are you telling me, your family hasn't given you the dates but they expect you to be there?"

"Welcome to the shit show." I raise my hands in defeat. "There's no telling these people no. It's unacceptable."

"Wow. Kind of glad I only have one sibling." He takes a moment to think about what I've said. "Why is it so critical that you're there?"

A million reasons jump to the top of my head. Because they want to control my life. Because they don't want me to be successful unless they have some sort of input in it. But that's not what I tell him.

"They still want me to be a part of the business. And, not just a voice. They want me to be hands on, and my heart isn't in it. Running a winery has never been my passion."

"Do they know that?"

As much as I want to say yes, they do, I'm not sure that's right. I've never explicitly told them I don't want a part in the business. I've only ever dodged their questions or given vague non-committal responses.

"I think so."

He reaches across the counter and places his hand on mine. "How important is it that you go on this trip?"

"According to my brother, it's very important."

"Okay, I'll go with you."

"But don't you have responsibilities with the band?"

"That's where you're in luck. We're actually on an extended break. The band is building a studio here, so I'll be here a bit helping with that."

"Oh my gosh. You are a lifesaver." I can't contain the smile taking over my face. "You don't know how much this means to me."

"Don't get too excited." He grins and I wonder if this is how he felt when I tried blackmailing him into going. "I have some stipulations of my own. Well, one really."

I remove my hand out from under his. "Like what? This whole thing is fake, there will be no actual feelings coming into play."

"Believe me, I know where you stand on relationships." He chuckles and I refuse to admit how much the sound warms my heart. "But, I want you to tell your family, out loud, that you don't want a place in the business."

Never in my life have I stood up to my parents. Not because I haven't wanted to, but because it's terrifying. Plus, my siblings would do everything in their power to keep it from happening. They love the family business, though. I don't know why they can't accept the fact I don't.

"I can try." An honest answer is what he deserves after offering to go with me.

"No." He shakes his head again. "You will. There's no

reason to tiptoe around your feelings because of something everyone else wants.”

“Is that why you keep trying to talk to me? You don’t avoid your feelings?”

His cheeks redden before he gathers his composure. “I know where I stand with you. I’m saying this as a friend.”

“Fine, fine.” I grumble and look away. “I’ll tell them point blank I don’t want to be a part of the business.”

“Can you say that a little louder? I didn’t quite hear you.” He taps his ear.

“I will tell my family I don’t want to work at the winery.” I hope he’s happy. “You realize you’re kind of annoying, right?”

“I’m annoyingly right? I know.” He glances around the counter. “Do you have a piece of paper?”

“Why?”

“So, you have my number when you find out the dates.”

Oh, duh. I look behind the counter where Emily keeps the notepads. We take most of our orders on the tablet or computers but she likes to write things down when she’s walking around the shop.

“Here you go.” I hand him a sticky note and pen.

“Thanks.” I watch him scribble his number on the paper before sliding it back to me. “So, can we get the order placed before they really can’t fit me in?”

“Shit. Yeah, sorry.” I pull out the tablet and open up the product page. “Does he have a certain style he wants?”

My focus may be on Tristan and the order he's plac-ing, but it doesn't mean I don't hear footsteps hightailing it down the hallway. If I were to place a bet, I'm guessing Kate was listening in to the entire conversation. I already know I'm going to catch hell for this.

"Well, aren't you a devious one?" Kate grins at me as I walk into the warehouse to let them know about the orders on order for tomorrow.

Emily glances up, confused. "What do you mean? Paula's probably the quietest person here. I don't see how she'd get a chance to *be* devious."

Looks like I was right. Kate was totally listening in on my conversation. My cheeks redden at being found out. Of all the people to hear what went down, it had to be her. I haven't known these women as long as they've known each other, but Kate is definitely nosy and likes to get the whole group involved.

"I don't know what you mean." I take a seat at the work table and glance down at the tablet in my hand. "There are four orders placed for tomorrow. They should show up in the list soon."

Kate snorts and I want her to drop it. "Did you really think that trade off was going to work?"

"I was hoping it would." I shrugged my shoulders. "Why did you even come up there anyway?"

She shrugs and tilts her head to the side. "You would have let anyone slide in an order past the due date.

You've done it for other occasions. I wanted to know why this one you would need our approval on. It was pure curiosity."

"And you happened to linger because…"

I grew up with five siblings, I know why she stuck around. Everyone likes a bit of gossip from those closest to them. Especially, when I'm not one that shares too much about my life. It's easier that way.

"Curiosity like I said." She grabs a flower and trims it down before placing it in a vase. "But, I am intrigued as to why he'd tell you to just ask. It's almost as if y'all know each other outside of listening to Crooked Halo at the bar."

Sam rolls her eyes and nudges Kate with her elbow. "She clearly doesn't want to talk about it, drop it." She glances at me. "Seriously, you don't have to tell us anything you don't want to. Kate seems to forget people have boundaries."

"No." Kate shakes her head. "I don't forget. I barge straight through them. We're a close-knit team, it's only fair that we know some details about each other."

"That's not what you were saying when Xander entered the picture." Emily laughs. "You shut us down at every line of questioning."

"We're not talking about me." Kate grumbles.

"It's fine." I wave the comments away. "We spent a night together a while a back. It's no big deal."

"That's how me and Xander met." Kate sighs, and a smile takes over her face. She really and truly is in love, and I'm happy she's found it.

"It wasn't exactly a one-night stand type of thing, though."

"What do you mean?" Emily asks.

I run through the events of the night, and when I look up at my coworkers, and friends, their eyes are wide. Disbelief written all over their faces.

"He also tried talking to me at Tiffany's wedding." I point to Emily since she's the one who saw him. "But, I completely blew him off. I don't understand why he'd offer to go on this trip with me."

"I do." Kate raises her hand as if she's in class.

"Enlighten me." I wave my hands over the table, a sign for her to give me the evidence.

"He's got it bad for you. It's the only explanation."

"No."

"Yes, the fact the one-night stand wasn't typical means he's invested. Looks like you'll end up in a relationship soon."

Shit. That's not what I want to hear at all, even if I have zero aspirations to be involved romantically with anyone.

tristan

TODAY WE BREAK ground on the studio. It's happening a lot faster than I anticipated. When you have a popular band as the owner of the property, I guess that moves things along at a faster speed. Or, this was in the works before they filled in the rest of the crew. Which is totally plausible.

Dale pulls me away from the rest of the group. "Did you get the flowers ordered?"

"Yep." I will not be elaborating on what else went down. I'm still trying to figure it out myself.

"They didn't charge you extra?"

"Not at all. It was the same price as they charge everyone else. We barely made the cut off time."

A small white lie won't be the end of all things.

"Good deal. You're a lifesaver, man." He pats me on the shoulder and turns to walk toward the rest of the group.

"Actually, I'll need off for a bit. I'm just not sure when."

"Anything you need." He waves the request away. "We're only working on the studio for the next few months. No tours or side gigs."

Damn. I guess I really need to look into a rental property. I'm still getting paid for helping out with the build and making sure everything is ready to go. It's one of the perks of working with them. As last minute as they can be with a lot of things, they take care of their crew.

"Not even an impromptu show at Out of the Ashes?"

"Well, I don't really consider that a side gig. At this point, it's like coming home."

He's not wrong. Who knew a rock band from the city would like spending so much time in a town so small. Definitely not me.

"Sounds like the next few months will be less chaotic."

"For sure." He nods in agreement. "It'll do us all some good to have down time."

"I'm still needed around, right?" Job security is something I never thought I'd need to think about with them since we're on the road so much, but being in one place for a long period of time could mean they won't need me here.

"Of course. Why wouldn't we? Every one of the crew will be here, and still get paid. Please, don't worry about that."

Whew. Thank God. Not that I can't go out and find

another job to carry me over, I don't want to. As inconvenient as some of the requests are, I love my job.

"That's a relief."

"Unless, of course, you're ready to move on."

"Not at all." I shake my head. How many people can say they get to tour the world with a popular band.

"Good. We'd hate to lose you." He continues toward the construction site. "If you don't want to stay at the house we're renting out, it may not be a bad idea to check out some local real estate. Especially since this will be home away from home."

"It's already on my list." I call out to his retreating back.

Now if Paula would let me know the dates of the family vacation, I can get it squared away. I can't believe I even agreed to do it. I wasn't lying when I told her all she had to do was ask. Putting my feelings aside may be another issue altogether.

"What can I get you?" Eric asks from behind the bar. I don't know why he thinks I'm going to order anything other than my usual whiskey and coke. It's my comfort drink.

"The usual." I glance around the bar to see if anyone I know has come in. So far, no such luck. I keep hoping I'll run into Paula. Though she probably doesn't want to see me yet.

"I hear you'll be in town for a bit," he says as he pours the whiskey into a glass.

"Yep. Dale suggested I start looking at property to rent or buy because it looks like this will be Crooked Halo's second home."

"That's good to hear. I love you guys."

"Um, thanks." It's hard to hear folks complement me like I'm part of the band. Knowing what I do as part of the crew is important, is completely different than accepting praise for it.

He finishes adding the coke and hands it over to me. "It'll be good to see you in here more often. Pretty much half the town comes in for lunch. You can get the small town feel like the locals."

"Thanks, man." I lift my drink in the air and slide some cash into the tip jar.

Taking a sip, I enjoy the perfection he has with this drink. It's the perfect balance all the way around.

The door opens and my eyes shift to the front of the building. Sadly, it wasn't Paula walking through the door. My shoulders sag, and I take another drink.

"Are you waiting for someone?" Eric asks as he pours a drink.

"Nope." I have to stop keeping an eye out for her. Any interest outside of our deal is off the table. She's made it more than clear where she stands on relationships.

"One of these days you guys will be honest with me when I ask that question." Eric shakes his head.

"What do you mean?"

He sighs before passing the drink to a waiting patron and leaning against the bar. "I know what it looks like to like someone and be waiting on their every appearance. Hell, it was me when my girl started working here."

"And you think that's what I look like?"

"No." He shakes his head. "I know. So, who's the lucky person?"

"Technically, we're not dating. At least, not for real."

"The plot thickens."

"I'm supposed to be her boyfriend on her trip with her family." I tap my glass against the bar top. "I may have bitten off more than I can chew."

"Wow, you're having doubts already and it hasn't even happened yet?"

"Not doubts about pulling it off, but keeping my feelings in check. I do like her. I have since I met her the first time in this bar. But, I've never been great at hiding how I feel."

That's the whole reason I was part of the stage crew in high school theatre. Schooling my facial expressions has never been easy. If I didn't come out and say what I was thinking, or feeling, my face would.

"So, you're really only doing this out of the goodness of your heart. You don't have ulterior motives?"

"No other reasoning. Despite what she thinks, I care about her happiness as a friend. Nobody should be ordered about the way her family seems to do."

Eric laughs and hits the top of the bar with his palm. "Good luck, man. She's going to eat you alive. And if she doesn't her family will."

"Are they really that bad?" Maybe this was a bad idea, and I've bitten off more than I can handle. It wouldn't be the first time. But...those usually involved the crew when I was in high school theatre. Thinking I can do more than I actually can isn't one of my best traits.

Eric doesn't answer right away, and it does nothing to quell the worry building in my stomach. He's the person I've learned to go to if I want information on anything. He may know more than the little old ladies I've seen gossiping when I come in for lunch on occasion. One of the perks of being a bartend, I guess. Everyone spills their guts at some point.

"It's not that they're bad." Finally, he speaks. "They are *very* involved. Or, at least, try to be. Paula doesn't make it easy for them."

"The rest of her siblings do whatever their parents tell them?"

I have an older brother, but he's much older. By the time I was getting to my annoying stage in life, he was off at college.

He shrugs. "Pretty much. They don't have a reason not to, and I think they really enjoy being a part of the business." He points over his shoulder. "We have a contract with them to sell their wine, and it flies off the shelves."

"Can you pour me a glass when I'm done?"

Who knows if I'll like it. I've never been a fan of wine. The after taste isn't my jam. Hopefully I'll be able to enjoy it. If not, things will be awkward on this vacation.

"Sure thing." Eric gives a quick wave and moves on to another customer.

I guess I was taking too much of his time. But when I glance around, I notice the bar has filled up. It's a shock he didn't bail on me sooner. Being too inside my thoughts is never a good thing, clearly. Most people don't pay so little attention to their surroundings as I do.

This whole thing with Paula is kind of a big deal. At least for her it is. The last thing I want to do is screw it up for her.

I gulp the rest of my drink. After this next glass, I'm done for the night. Hopefully I can call one of the guys to give me a ride home.

Before my glass hits the counter, Eric is sliding a wine glass toward me. "Here you go, I took the liberty of choosing a flavor for you."

"Thanks." I nod at him. Him picking out the wine is good thing because I can't tell the difference between each one.

Studying the glass, I lift it to my lips and take a small sip. As soon as the liquid hits my tongue, I expect to want to spit it out, but I don't. It's sweet with a touch of a tang I can't quite place.

I take a bigger drink in case the first one was a fluke, and I was forcing myself to enjoy it. But it wasn't. It's really good. Who would have thought I'd be into wine. Well, this one specifically. I make a mental note to ask Eric which kind it is.

"That better be made by my family."

I choke on the wine at the sound of her voice. How does she manage to sneak up on me like that? I'll have to ask her as soon as I know I'll live through this coughing fit.

CHAPTER FIVE

OH MY GOD. Is he dying? I pat his back. I don't know why it's a gut reaction. Also, I'm pretty sure my mom did the same thing when I was a kid and having a choking fit. Or well, coughing, I guess.

"Tristan?" I try to lean over until I can see his face, but there's a good chance we'll bump heads.

He holds up a finger while trying to gain his composure. So, not dying. That's good at least. My cheeks are probably bright red, and I can feel everyone in the bar staring at us.

"Damn, Paula." I glance over the bar to see Eric studying the situation. "I thought your family was going to take him out, not you."

"I didn't do it on purpose."

"I know." Eric grins. "Tristan, do we need to call someone to come help you out?"

He shakes his head back and forth. "I—just—need—a minute."

His voice is raspy between coughs, and I feel even worse. After this, he may not want to help me out anymore.

"I'm gonna hang around just in case," Eric says as he leans against the bar. "You know, your family isn't going to believe you're dating if you don't show up to spaces together."

"You know about our arrangement?"

"Yep." he nods. "I'm a bartender. I pull out all the best secrets."

I watch Tristan pick up the glass and take a drink before clearing his throat. He's okay. "Don't act like you coerced me into saying anything. I did that of my own volition."

"You told him?" This shouldn't be shocking, but it is. I figured he found out from Caroline or one of my other coworkers.

"Yeah." He takes another sip. Water would probably be better, and before I can voice my thought, Eric is sliding a glass across the counter. "Thanks. I wanted to see if he knew anything about your family."

"You could have asked me." Though I'd probably start ranting. They aren't bad, just annoying. It's probably best it came from an outside party.

"I know. And I will because we'll need to get some key facts straight. Do you have a date, yet?"

"Yeah, two weeks from tomorrow." Dread fills my stomach already and it's not even time to leave on this trip.

"Wow." He shakes his head. "They really don't give you a lot of notice."

He's not wrong. It's completely normal, though. They plan something and expect everyone to move their schedules around to accommodate them. It's actually pretty unfair.

"If you can't make it, I totally understand." Everything inside of me is hoping he can still go with me. I can endure my family alone, but why do it if I don't have to.

"It should be fine. Dale told me to let him know the dates."

Phew. The tension inside my body melts away with these few words.

"I guess it's a good thing we have understanding bosses."

"Yep. It helps that we aren't touring right now. Otherwise..."

He lets the words drift off because that means I would be on my own, and he doesn't want to voice it.

"Well, I'm glad I ran into you."

He shoots a quick glance at Eric, and his cheeks blush. "Why's that?"

"So, I could tell you the dates. Even though I'm pretty sure I also almost killed you."

"Naw." He waves me off. "It went down the wrong pipe is all."

Eric is shaking his head but doesn't say anything else. What does he know that I don't? Pressing him for information later is now at the top of my to-do list.

"You want the usual, Paula?" He has the audacity to smile at me like he isn't holding some sort of secret.

"Sure." I turn back to Tristan. "Since we're here, do you want to start going over all my family stuff and how we *got together*?" I do air quotes with those last to words. "Unless, you have something else to do, of course."

Why in the hell am I being so weird? Talking to guys has never been an issue for me. But the briefest interactions with Tristan bring out a side of me I didn't realize I had.

"No, I'm good to hang around." Relief passes over his face, and I wonder why he doesn't want to leave yet. But...it's not my business. He'll tell me if he feels like it.

"Here you go." Eric slides my margarita across the counter. "There's a table over there they finished cleaning. I'll let Delilah know y'all are heading that way."

"Thanks." I salute him with my glass before heading in the direction he pointed. Hopefully Tristan is following because if we don't snag it, someone else will. The bar is crowded tonight, but not so much there's a wait for tables. If there was, I'd feel terrible Eric told us to take this one.

I set my glass on the table and lift myself into the tall chair. Honestly, I think bars should do away with high tables with chairs. It's practically asking for someone to fall off it in a drunken stupor. Or, even sober. I can't count how many times I've lost my balance sliding down, and I'm not even that short.

Tristan takes the seat across from me. The glass of wine still in his hand.

"So, was it my family wine you were drinking?"

He glances at the glass as if he forgot he still had it. "Oh, yeah. I figured it was best if I at least tried it before going on this trip with you. I'm not typically a wine drinker, but this is good."

At least he likes the product. "Which kind did you order?"

"I actually have no idea." He laughs.

"What?" How do you not know what you're ordering? That feels like a crime.

"I told Eric to pick for me, and this is what he gave me."

I hold out my hand toward him. "Let me take a sip. I can tell you which one it is."

He looks from the glass to me. "Um, okay."

Oh no. I hope he's not someone who doesn't like germs. Not because it's bad or anything, but because I basically just demanded his drink.

"It's okay. I'll ask Eric later."

"No, no, it's fine." He places the glass in my hand, and waits for my assessment.

The scent alone clues me on which kind it is. But I take a small sip to make sure I'm right. I'm much like Tristan in that I don't drink a lot of wine. Being surrounded by it my entire life kind of made me hate it on principle.

"No wonder you like this one. It's our sangria. Super sweet but will knock you on your ass if you're not careful."

He grins at me, and butterflies swirl around my stomach.

"So, what you're saying is I should probably stop after this glass." He takes it back and takes a sip.

Well, at least I know he doesn't have a problem drinking after me. Though we're going to need to figure out the PDA aspect of our relationship. My parents are never going to believe we're together if we never touch.

"Are there any questions you have about the trip?"

"In general, or specific?"

"Both?" I know we need to get the specifics squared away. The family will understand if he doesn't know everything about them. They probably assume I never talk about them since I don't want to be a part of the business.

"We probably need to figure out how we started dating."

"Easy, we use the story of how we met when you knocked the phone out of my hand." It's not a complete lie. He did in fact go home with me that night. Even if the night didn't go as I intended.

"And the reason folks haven't seen us around together is because I've been on tour with the band. So, it's not completely impossible for us to have been dating."

"Exactly." It's one of the reasons he's the perfect person to be my fake boyfriend for this trip. He's only around when the band is. And it's not like I come to this bar that much outside of girl's night.

"Now that we have that detail out of the way. How much shit is your family going to give you...and me?"

"It depends on their mood. I haven't told them I'm bringing a plus one yet."

"Oh." He cocks his head to the side. "So, they're going to hate me right off the bat."

"Not at all. I'll tell them tomorrow." I take a sip of my now melting margarita. "How much touching are we okay with?"

He's once again choking on his drink. I give him a few moments to regain his composure.

"You've gotta stop surprising me like that."

"It's not like it's an invalid question." I shrug as if it's no big deal. But it is. He's the only guy who I've ever been interested in and we've never even kissed.

"Definitely hand holding." He studies his empty glass as if it holds all the answers. "I'm assuming we'll need to kiss on occasion."

"Most likely. And we'll probably be sharing a room. My parents aren't old fashioned in their way of thinking."

Tristan's eyes widen. I guess he didn't think about that particular detail. And there isn't time to find a place bigger with more rooms. They always rent a house wherever we go so we can have *quality* bonding time.

"As long as there are extra blankets, I can sleep on the floor."

"Don't be ridiculous." I wave away his concern. "At some point before we leave, we'll have to practice kissing, though. It needs to be believable. If not, my siblings will know."

"That's actually kind of creepy."

"You don't have any siblings, do you?"

"A brother, but we didn't really grow up together since he's so much older."

That makes sense. "So, you didn't get the siblings all up in your business action I did."

"Nope." He shakes his head. "But...were you in their business as well?"

"I plead the fifth." Yes, yes, I was. Nothing happened in that house without me knowing about it. Though that changed some when I moved out and the younger siblings were still in school.

"Is there any other pertinent information I need to know?"

I'm glad he doesn't make me elaborate. He must know good and well that I was nosey.

"Not really. My great-grandparents started the winery and passed it down. I actually think I'm the first one that hasn't wanted anything to do with it. No disrespect to my family, but it's not something I've ever wanted to do."

"Okay, cool." His whole body sags in relief. "I mean I'm pretty good at memorizing things quickly from when I was in theatre, but it's good I don't have to. But it'd be helpful if you sent me pictures of everyone and their names so I get that right at least."

"I can do that."

The shift in conversation feels like our evening of

drinks is winding down. He proves my point when he slides out of his chair. "I probably need to get back to the house so I can let Dale know the dates and see what he has on the agenda for me tomorrow."

"Okay." I turn to carefully get out of my chair, but his hand appears in front of me to help. "Thanks."

My voice is barely above a whisper. He must hear it, though. He nods his head with a half-smile.

"Any time."

"I need to close out my tab."

"Don't worry about it. I'll take care of it."

"You don't have—"

"I can't let my girlfriend pay for her own drinks. How would that make me look to the fine residents of Asheville?"

There's no use arguing, and it's been a while since anyone has bought me a drink. I follow him to the bar to take care of the bill. Even though we aren't really together, I don't want the night to end. It's been a long time since I've felt this comfortable with anyone.

Once he's finished up, he leads the way out of the bar, and I pull my arms around myself to stave off the cold. He wraps an arm around me and pulls me closer to him.

"Where are you parked?"

I nod in the direction of my car and we head toward it. He waits until I've unlocked the car and opened the door before pulling his arm away.

"Tonight was fun. Even if there was a bit of homework." He shoves his hand in his pocket and rocks back and forth.

"It was. I'm glad I ran into you." And almost killed him, but I don't want to mention that again. "So, uh, do we want to practice the kiss? I mean, no time like the present, right?"

"Sure." He takes a step toward me and places his hand on my cheek before leaning in.

HIs mouth meets mine, and I only expected a sweet peck. That's not at all what's happening here.

His lips are soft and he widens them a fraction to deepen the kiss. I wrap my arms around his waist and melt into him. Standing here, kissing him, feels like the only thing that matters. The bitter bite of winter fades away. All I can do is stay wrapped up in this warmth.

I'm not sure how long we kiss, but when he pulls away reality comes crashing back.

"Was that, okay?" He sounds unsure of himself.

"Yeah." It's not my fault if I sound like I'm out of breath. He stole it from me. "It was perfect."

"Text me when you get home?"

"Uh huh." I wait a beat. "I'll also send the pictures."

With a quick wave he turns around and walks off. I am so screwed.

tristan

MY MIND IS STILL STUCK on the kiss with Paula. I didn't mean for it to be as elaborate as it was. Something came over me and it felt right. Based on her reaction she was okay with it as well.

We've texted here and there. Mostly her filling me on things she forgot about. However, the kiss has not been mentioned. It's a shame because I'd like to know what she really thought. Was she as into it as it seemed? Or, was it merely practice for how she needs to react when I kiss her around her family?

"Do we need to go over the siblings again?" Dale asks, breaking me from my thoughts.

"No, I think I've got it." It's all I've been studying for the past week. This whole relationship thing is a farce, I know that. But I don't want to show up to her family vacation looking like an idiot. They'll never believe we're together.

Dale looks around the construction area to make sure

we're alone. "Are the flowers all set to be delivered tomorrow?"

"Yep. Paula said to give her a time, and they'd try to get them too as close to it as possible."

"Can you tell her around 6:30 tomorrow night?"

"Sure. Where at?"

"Here." He nods toward the studio being built.

"It's not even done, yet."

"Not in the studio." He laughs before pointing to the house. "In there. I'm going to set it up in the morning. I made sure there wasn't anything wrong with the plumbing or electrical yesterday."

That bit of information is shocking. That's normally something I would do. He hands off all those tasks to me. Maybe he's practicing for the week I'll be gone. Either way, it still kind of hurts that he didn't put me in charge of that.

"That's great."

"Yeah. Speaking of, I'll need you to distract her while I spend time out here getting everything set up."

"Why do I have to distract her?"

Not that I'm not capable, but it feels weird to have me do it.

"Well, not just her."

Good gravy. I would have rather dealt with the utility people. How in the hell did I get turned into a glorified babysitter?

"I'll lead them in a particular direction then I'll leave them to their own devices."

He sighs, but knows he's asked too much of me.

"Actually, we may send them to Dallas for a bit. Tell them we need them to pick out some stuff for the studio. It's not technically a lie."

"See two birds one stone." This is an option I'm encouraging because as much as I love everyone, it's not how I want to spend my day.

"I don't know why I didn't think of that before."

"Glad you figured it out." And it means I'm off the hook for entertaining people for the day. Besides at some point today I need to start packing and looking for a place to stay while we're here.

Even though I doubt things will progress past friendship with Paula, I don't want to hang out with her in a house full of band members. They aren't bad to hang out with…but they have a tendency to be loud for no reason. There's always an instrument being played or random signing throughout the house.

Honestly, it's a lot like how it was when I hung out with my theatre crew in high school. Now that I think about it, it's probably the reason I feel so comfortable there. But alone time is a necessity. I know Paula has been around a loud intruding family most of her life, but it seems like it's not what she likes to surround herself with at this point in time.

"Let's get some of this stuff done."

I have no clue what he's talking about, but I'll do whatever he points out. Most of the work on the studio is being done by the construction crew. There are things in the house that most likely need to be done, especially with his big event planned for this evening. Hopefully it all turns out great for him. I know his girlfriend will love it no matter what he does.

The bell above the door of Whoopsie Daisy rings as I struggle to open it. The bags are awkward to hold as I shove my way through. The group of people hovering around the counter tells me this is probably a bad idea. I definitely should have called before I showed up with food.

Both Paula and Emily are taking care of folks at the counter, and I hang back until they get through as many people as they can. I knew Valentine's Day would be busy for them, but I never thought they'd be slammed like this.

People seem to go all out on showing their partners they care about them this one day during the year. Maybe they should do it year-round so they don't have to run themselves ragged.

From the outside looking in, it might seem like I'm hating on them, but I'm not. I've never been in a serious relationship during this holiday. Or in a while to be perfectly honest. Getting burned by one person too many will do that to a guy.

"What are you doing here?" Paula's voice breaks through my thoughts.

Shaking my head to snap out of the state of my love life, I smile and lift up the bags.

"You said you hadn't had a chance to eat. I'm here to remedy that."

She eyes almost bursting bags. "Did you buy the whole restaurant to feed me?"

"No." I readjust my hold on the handles. "I figured if you hadn't eaten, nobody else had either. I just hope it's enough food for everyone."

Paula glances to Emily and has some sort of silent conversation. After a few seconds, she moves to an area of the counter and lifts it up. She nods for me to come back, and I do. She closes the counter and moves to my side before sidling up next to me.

"You didn't have to do this." She points to the bags in my hands.

Worry that I've overstepped gnaws at me. I have a feeling most people in her family haven't done anything to help Paula. At least, not without it pertaining to the business.

"I know. But you said you hadn't eaten, and you didn't know when you'd get a chance to grab lunch." I hold up the bag in question. "Now you don't have to think about it."

"Thanks." The hallway isn't as bright as the front of the store, and I wish I could see her expression clearly.

"You're welcome." I want to do everything in my power to show her that people can do kind things without expecting something in return.

We enter the chaos of the back room. It's spacious and there are rows of refrigeration units along with shelves of various vases, wreaths, and other items they may need to create their floral designs.

"Lunch is served," Paula calls out. The two other women who own the shop glance up and a man I've seen in Out of the Ashes quite a bit stands.

"Who is the angel that's graced us with a feast?" The blonde woman asks and places her hand over her heart. By the dramatics, you'd think she was in theatre in a past life. She certainly has the flare for it.

"I'm Tristan, Paula's...friend." It feels like settling on a word, but that's what we are. Friends.

"Oh, right." She drawls out. "I'm Kate and this is Samantha. I'm sure you've seen Emily up front. And this is my brother Kai."

"Sup, Man." He lifts a hand in acknowledgment. "You saved me a call. I was going to order food in a bit. We're slammed today."

"No problem." I nod in his direction. "I figured if Paula hadn't eaten yet, y'all haven't either. I hope I got enough."

Kai walks toward me and offers to take one of the bags. "We can set them up on the table over here."

I follow him to the table, but I don't miss the raised eyebrows on Kate's face as she rushes toward Paula. What exactly has she told them about me?

"I hope y'all have plates or something. I didn't grab any."

"Yeah, we have some in the kitchen, which is probably a better place to set this up, but today we need to be able to eat while we work. There are too many orders that need to go out.”

“Understandable. There’s a few different types of tacos. It was the most variety I could get for the price. I wasn’t sure how many employees there are.”

“It’s just us most of the time. The drivers come in and out, of course. They’ll be excited about the food.”

“Good. Anything to make it easier on you guys. Especially after squeezing in the order for Dale.”

“That’s where I’ve seen you.” Kai snaps his fingers. “You work with Crooked Halo. And I think I saw you at Tiffany’s wedding.”

“Yeah.” I shrug. “I go pretty much anywhere the band goes. I’m part of the road crew.”

“That’s a pretty cool gig.”

“It allows me to see a lot of places.”

“Let me grab the plates and napkins.” Kai backs up. “It shouldn’t take long.”

I finish setting out the styrofoam containers holding the various tacos. Thank God the restaurant labeled them. I would have never been able to tell one from the other. But I know they’re good. We’ve eaten there a few times while in town.

“I can see you’ve made friends with my coworkers.” Paula is beside me, scoping out the options. “They don’t let too many people into their circle so if they like you, I know my family will.”

“Speaking of, where are we going?” I probably should have gotten that information when she told me the dates.

"Oh, um, the beach."

"In the middle of winter?" It feels like an odd choice for the time of year.

Paula rolls her eyes and sighs. "Yep. They said because it's less busy. Besides Winter is subjective when we live in Texas. One day it can be eighty degrees and the next forty."

"You're right." It's one of the things that makes living in this area annoying. The weather can't ever decide what it's going to do. "So, I basically need to pack for anything that can happen."

"Pretty much." She grabs a taco, unwraps the foil and takes a bite. I can't take my eyes off her lips. Watching her eat is definitely weird, but it makes me wonder if she thinks about the kiss we shared as much as I do.

"What's up with all the weird looks the women of the shop are giving me?"

"Nothing." She blurts out almost dropping her food. She takes a moment to regain her composure. "They are just being weird."

I shift to the side and glance over her shoulder. The women in question are staring at us with silly grins on their faces. As soon as they realize I've spotted them, they make themselves look busy.

Paula definitely said something to them, and I hope to find out what while we're on our trip. But I don't want to be the one to bring it up. I guess time will tell.

CHAPTER SEVEN

"WE'RE HERE." Tristan says. His voice is only slightly above a whisper as he stares at the beach house in front of us.

Rock music is playing softly from the speakers. I shouldn't be surprised at his choice in tunes considering the band he works for. We spent most of the drive fine tuning the details of us so there aren't any holes in our story.

The times we weren't talking, we rode in companionable silence. It wasn't awkward like I thought it would be. Both of us were probably lost in our own thoughts and anxieties about what the week might bring.

"Should we get out?" I ask without making a move for the door handle.

I know we have these vacations every year, but this is first time I've felt stress about it. They've been pressuring me more than ever to have a role in the company. But I've also never introduced them to anyone. Much less a person who isn't even actually my boyfriend. We have to pull this off. Once we're back home, we'll *end* things and all will be back to normal.

"You know we could always see if there are other beach houses available for rent. Or even a hotel."

He's just as nervous as I am. At least I know I'm not alone in the feeling. It's a little ridiculous to have this emotion around my own family, but it can't be helped. They've done this to me. I used to love being around them until they started demanding an answer any time we're together.

"As much as I'd love to run away with you, I don't think we can."

I point to the curtain moving, and also realize what I just said. I think that may have been a little too close to the truth. Since that kiss, and all the messages we've shared back and forth, he's become my favorite person to talk to.

"I mean, run away from my family with you. Not actually run away with you." Cringing I cover my face with my hands. There's no way the explanation made things any better.

Tristan pulls my hands away from my face and smiles. "Keep telling yourself that. You may find running away with me would be fun."

He turns off my car, opens the door and hurries out of the car. Before I can ask him what he's doing, he's at my door, pulling the handle. With a deep breath, I unbuckle my seatbelt and rest my hand in the one he's offering.

Now that I'm out of the car, I realize it's cooler here than expected. Like I told him before, Texas weather will always get the best of us. He wraps his arm around my waist, pulling me closer to his warmth as he closes the car door.

"Should I get the bags now, or wait?"

"Wait." I tell him. "Maybe we'll get lucky and they'll tell us to stay somewhere else."

"Your parents can't honestly be that bad."

"They aren't." Not really. They are some of the kindest people, and constantly host benefits at the winery. They just like to needle me, and don't like the honest reactions I give them.

He pulls his arm out from around me and slides his hand into mine. "We've got this. If push comes to shove, we can leave. It's not like they can force us to stay here."

"No, but they can shame us if we decide it's too much and want to leave."

"I guess it's a good thing I'm shameless."

He grins and takes a step forward. Then another. I trudge along beside him, psyching myself up to deal with the barrage of questions, and probable disaster that will come from being here.

It doesn't take us long to get to the door. The stairs are a bit worse for wear, but nothing I'm not used to. He raises his hand to knock, but the door opens before it can connect. How do they do that?

"You're finally here." My mom holds her arms out and pulls me into a hug. My hand releases from Tristan's, and the grounding I felt moments ago disappears. The anxiety I have when I'm around my parents, comes back in full force. "It's a shame we don't see you more often considering we live in the same town."

There it is. Not even a minute has gone by without her adding a passive aggressive comment. I'm not sure what she thinks it will accomplish. There's a reason I rarely go to their house. They never show interest in what I like to do unless it pertains to how it can benefit the family business. Work is what it *always* boils down to.

"Hi, Mom." I grumble. "Where is everyone?"

"Your brothers made a run to get some drinks and food. Your sister is in the living room with your dad."

"Oh, cool." Not cool at all. It means they'll block in my car and I won't have an escape plan should I need it.

"And who is this?" Mom's eyes focus on my companion for this hellish experience.

"Mom, this is Tristan. Tristan, this is my mom, Abigail."

Moving to the side, I let them exchange pleasantries. I study mom to see what she's going to do. She's naturally a hugger unless she doesn't like you. Then she'll slide her hand out in front of her and shakes hands as quickly as possible. Most people don't even notice the snub.

She swoops in for a hug. "I didn't realize you were bringing someone with you."

Tristan's head whips toward me, eyes wide, as he pulls out of the embrace. He didn't want to be a surprise guest, and he wasn't.

"Mom, I messaged you last week about him coming with me."

"Oh." She waves my words away. "I didn't think you were serious. We don't have an extra bed for him."

Unbelievable. It takes everything in me not to throw my hands in the air in frustration. Mostly because I don't want to be scolded like a child.

"That's fine." It's my turn to push her concern aside. "Seeing as he's my boyfriend we only need the one."

A part of me expects her freak out. She's never really been old fashioned when it comes to us sleeping in the same room as the person we're dating. I mean, at this point, we're all adults. But she likes to show her disappointment in me at every turn, and this is one of those moments she can do that.

"Oh, okay then." She steps to the side of the door. "Come inside. It's cold out there."

Both of us take a step at the same time. Our motions completely in sync, and it's honestly a little weird. I don't even have that sort of timing with my siblings.

"Where are your bags?" Mom's attention is on our empty hands.

"I'll get them in a bit. We weren't sure anyone was here and didn't want to lug them back and forth." Tristan's smile is endearing, but I know the real reason he didn't get them out. It was a chance to bail out should the need arise. He wants to take stock of the situation in case we need to bail.

"Okay." Mom takes his answer at face value. "Let's

get these introductions out of the way, though you'll have another round once the boys get back."

"Why did Piper stay home?" I ask as we walk from the entryway by the kitchen to the living room. This house has a pretty open floor plan, and is similar to other houses we've stayed in down here. I guess the house we normally rent wasn't available.

"Honestly, I think she's tired of your brothers' shenanigans." She shakes her head and grins. "They've been playing pranks on each other since they got here this morning."

"You can't just tell half the story, Mom." My sister calls back. "They all ganged up on me and tried to throw me in the ocean."

"We are in fact at the beach, Little Sister."

"In the *winter*." She growls. "They've lost their damn minds."

Picturing our brothers swoop in and carry down the beach is comical, but I'm sure she fought like hell. They probably have bruises to show for it.

Piper turns around and her eyes go round. "Who is this?"

Tristan lifts his hand in the air and gives a little wave. "I'm Paula's boyfriend, Tristan."

"How did I not know you had a boyfriend?" She screeches and climbs over the sofa to get to us. She wraps him in a hug and sways back and forth. "This is so exciting."

"It's news to all of us." Mom cuts her eyes toward me and I know we'll have a discussion about this later.

Finally, my sister lets go of him. "Welcome to the circus. I hope you're prepared."

Great. With that stunning endorsement he'll ditch me and haul ass back to Asheville. Not that I'd blame him. If I could, I'd join right along with him.

"If it's anything like my theatre group in high school, I'm sure I'll be just fine."

Well, at least he's not leaving. I was never in theatre in high school, and don't have anything to compare my family to, but I hope he means that.

"I'm glad you made it, kiddo." Dad is beside me and wrapping me into one of his infamous bear hugs. As much as I hate that he wants me to be a part of the winery, this is one of my favorite things about him. It makes me feel like I'm a kid again.

"Thanks, Daddy." I squeeze him back. "Sounds like we missed the chaos this morning."

"Yep. It was entertaining." He ignores the glare coming from his youngest child. "I only wish we caught it on camera."

"That would have been nice." I agree.

He lets go of me and holds out a hand. "I'm Paul, her dad."

"I gathered that." Tristan smiles. "Tristan, her boyfriend."

"Apparently." Dad's voice is gruff as if he doesn't approve. But last I checked, I'm a grown woman. I can have a boyfriend if I want.

"It's nice to meet you, Sir." His grip is still on my dad's hand. He's not letting go first. I applaud his bravery, but Dad doesn't back down easily. "Is Paula named after you?"

Now Dad is grinning and finally pulls his hand back. "As a matter of fact, she is."

"Oh God." My sister rolls her eyes and heads back to the sofa. "Here we go with the naming story for the millionth time."

As much as I'd like to join her and skip out on story time, I can't leave Tristan to fend for himself. Though, he's doing a pretty good job of winning my parents over. Well, Dad, at least. Mom is still on the fence. I can tell by the way she's studying him and judging whether or not he's good enough for me.

"When our oldest, Pierce, was born, she said I couldn't name him after me. She didn't want to have a Paul Junior running around. I let it go, and she named him. Gotta keep the wife happy." He tilts his head in an "am I right" gesture.

Tristan, to his credit, is engaged with the story. He's listening intently, as if it's the most important tale in the universe.

"So, when Paula was born, it was my turn to name a kid." He glances at Mom as if she wasn't there when he named me. "One of my kids was going to have my name-sake if I could manage it. So, I named her Paula. It's not a junior, but still a derivative of my name."

"That's actually genius, Sir." Tristan nods along with my dad. "I'll have to remember that for the future."

"Don't get any ideas." I shake my head. I know he's playing along with our relationship, but seriously, if he tries to name one of our imaginary future kids, Tristina, I might murder him.

My mom's gaze lands on me. She's not down for this idea either. Whether it's because she doesn't want things to last between us, or she doesn't believe we're together, I don't know. It's best to leave that conversation for another time.

"Let's finish the game. The boys should be back with the food soon." Dad gestures for Tristan to follow him.

He does. Just like that, Dad has brought him into the fold. Mom reaches for me, but I side step her and follow the others to the sofa.

I don't know who is playing, and don't really care. Basketball isn't a sport I care about. Or any sport for that matter. But it's nice spending time with him without bickering over my responsibilities to carry on the family business.

One of the teams scores and my dad cheers them on. I'll never understand this type of fandom. Grunts and laughter break through the celebration. When I turn around, my brothers are standing in the kitchen with a number of bags in their hands.

All of them are focused on Tristan. Tonight is about to get interesting. Hopefully Dad has his phone ready to record.

CHAPTER EIGHT

tristan

I DON'T KNOW why Paula is so put off by her family. They seem really nice. For a second, I thought I was going to lose my hand to her Dad, but my quick thinking put us on an upward trajectory. At least, I think it did. He didn't attempt to kick me out of the beach house.

Paula moves, and I catch it out of the corner of my eye. What in the world caught her attention?

Then I feel it. The awareness that people are staring at you, and you don't know why, or what to do about it. Slowly, I turn toward the back of the couch. Four guys have their focus on me. All but one are scowling at me. The one has a smirk on his face, and I can tell he's waiting to see where this goes. I guess introductions aren't quite over yet.

"Who the fuck are you?" One of the guys asks.

My mind goes back to the notes Paula sent me on her siblings, trying to remember which one this is. I guess nobody got the memo I was coming. Maybe Paula didn't send the text to her parents like she said. Or, they didn't think she'd actually bring me. Either way, this trip has been interesting from the jump.

"Don't be rude." Paula's mom moves over to her sons. "This is Paula's boyfriend, Tristan."

"What?" Pierce, I think he's the oldest one, shouts before dropping the bags in his hands.

"I hope there weren't eggs in there," Piper whispers and laughs.

Apparently, it was loud enough for Pierce to hear because he glares at her before returning his focus to me.

"I wasn't aware we were allowed to bring guests on this trip." His eyes never leave me, and I honestly wonder if I should be scared.

"Your sister told me last week," Abigail answers. "It slipped my mind."

The frustration is leaking from him. I don't even know this guy. Why does he have so much beef with a literal stranger?

Standing I take a few steps until I'm around the sofa and a couple of feet from the group of men taking stock of me. I hold out my hand. One of us has to make the first move and I refuse to be intimidated. I put up with way worse when I was in high school. Being bullied isn't how this will go down.

The brother who was smirking a few moments ago, takes a step forward and slides his hand in mine. "I'm Parker. It's good to meet you, Tristan." He glances over his shoulder as he releases the greeting. "Don't worry about them, they are more bark than bite."

So, he says. The other three look like they want to pummel me. Not that I blame them. Based on the reaction of everyone here, Paula doesn't bring guys around much, if at all. It has to be a shock to the status quo.

"Nice to meet you, Parker. Paula's told me a lot about you."

It's not a lie, I think he might be her favorite brother. Maybe it's his devil may care attitude, I don't know. But I also like him instantly. He's the least commanding of his siblings, and it means a lot that he stepped out when the others were looking to each other on what step to take next. It seems like he has a mind of his own.

"Of course she did. I'm the most charming brother." That comment earns a groan from all the siblings, including the sisters behind me. He definitely has charisma, I'll give him that. It probably also gets him in trouble.

He points to the brothers still in front of us, starting with the one he was standing beside. "That's Phillip, Peter, and the big ol' teddy bear is, Pierce."

"Stop fucking calling me that," Pierce mutters. His mom doesn't correct him this time.

Phillip gives a small wave now that he's not the first to make an introduction. Peter and Pierce are still trying to stab me with their glares.

"He may act like a hard ass, but he's a softie on the inside." Parker holds his hand to his chest like he's giving a vow.

"That's not even remotely true." Paula pipes in. "He's an asshole."

"Don't start." He throws in her direction.

Seriously, he thinks he can talk to her like that. I take a step and feel a touch on my arm. Paula is leaning over the sofa to get my attention, and gives a small shake of her head. Fine, I'll stand down this time, but the next time he's rude to her, I won't allow it.

"So do y'all always line up in age order?" The question slips out before I realize it. At this point, I'm hoping it'll ease the tension built up in the room. Everything was fine and pleasant before her brothers showed up.

"Not on purpose." Phillip sighs. "It started out as a way to do a head count when we were on vacation, and I guess it stuck."

"So, you know our ages, but not our names?" Peter's voice is laced with annoyance. I wouldn't be surprised if he's spent his whole life trying to impress his big brother. Maybe one day he'll realize being salty won't give him the validation he's searching for.

Is it an asshole move to be judging them while they're standing in front of me? Maybe, but I can't help it. Analyzing people is how I adjust my own interactions.

"I know your names, but they all start with P. I didn't want to screw it up and look dumb." Not completely a lie. They're all a bit older than the photos Paula showed me. But mostly it's so I can remember how each of them behave.

"That actually makes sense." Peter agrees. He sets his

bags on the table and moves toward me, slapping his hand in mine. "Nice to meet you, Tristan."

Well, at least I have three of her siblings on my side. It'd be nice to have all five of them, but I'll be fine with the majority.

"You too, man."

Abigail takes the bags from the eldest brother, and sets them on the counter before digging through them. "Did y'all get any actual food?"

"You shouldn't have sent us to the store. And the rest of them shouldn't have put me in charge of filling the basket with food while they got drinks." Parker shrugs and slides around me to sit on the sofa. I don't want to be stuck with Phillip and Pierce so I follow him and take my place beside Paula.

"I think that went pretty well." My words are a whisper and I hope she's the only one who can hear me.

"If that's what you call it." She snuggles into my side. Part of me wonders if this is part of the act, or if it's real. It can't be. She's already said multiple times she's not looking for a boyfriend. Except...this *feels* right.

* * *

"I didn't think we'd get a room to ourselves." I set my bag next to the dresser in the small space.

"Well, I usually share with Piper." Paula digs through her bag. "Since you're here, she's taking one of the bunks."

"Now I feel terrible. I'll sleep out there with your brothers. How is that fair to your sister?"

She shrugs and pulls out a top and some shorts. "Both of us agreed it's probably safer if you didn't."

A pit of dread fills my stomach. "Why? Are they going to feed me to the fishes?"

A bubble of laughter bursts from her lips. It's becoming one of my favorite sounds. As annoyed as she can get, and seem uptight at times, she is not afraid to live in the moment. Not giving a single damn about who can hear her joy.

"If they got the chance...maybe." My eyes widen at the seriousness in her voice. "I'm just kidding. But they do like to play pranks on people. Especially those they think they can push around."

"Parker seemed to like me just fine."

"Are you kidding me? He's the biggest prankster of them all. You'd think it wouldn't be so bad because he's one of the youngest, but he was a terror growing up. And that's coming from someone considerably older than him."

That doesn't fill me with confidence. Was his solidarity all for show? Maybe he's biding his time to pounce.

"You're making me happy I didn't 'grow up' with my brother. I can't imagine stuff happening to me all the time."

"It wasn't all the time." She rolls her eyes. "At least, not with me. He tended to pick on the rest of the boys more than me and Piper."

"Why?"

"Because we would snitch. Or I'd hit him. It was a toss-up on what the outcome would be."

"Remind me not to piss you off."

"For your information, I'm only like that with my siblings. It's totally normal."

"If you say so."

She moves to the door and cracks it open before peering down the hallway. "Ugh, I swear my sister takes a million years in the bathroom."

"You can always go to your parents room, if you have to use the restroom that bad."

"I just need to change." She closes the door and leans against it. "Can you turn around?" She twirls her finger in a circle to mimic the action.

"Sure." I do as she asks. There's nothing more appealing than staring at an off-white wall. "What are we going to do the rest of the time we're here? I mean it's not like any of the attractions are open in the dead of Winter."

"I'm sure my mom has a whole itinerary for us." She says as I hear a garment hit the floor.

"Oh." So they are that kind of family. The one who does everything together and know pretty much everything about each other. There probably aren't many secrets.

"Don't worry." She grunts. Another piece of clothing on the floor. "I won't leave you alone with them. I wouldn't do that to my worst enemy."

"So, I'm not an enemy?"

"If you were, I wouldn't have invited you. You're a... friend."

Friend. The word I'm coming to loathe. I know it's what we are, but based on the amount of texting we've done since she asked to participate in this farce, I was hoping maybe it would be a bit more than that.

"Okay, I'm done." She's bent over picking up her discarded clothes from the floor.

This woman is going to fucking kill me. The shorts barely cover her ass. The shirt hugs every curve of her body. She expects me to sleep next to her like that?

"Let me grab some pillows and a blanket. I'm sleeping on the floor."

"You don't have to do that." She scrunches her eyebrows together.

My gaze travels up and down her body. She doesn't realize how tempting it is to crawl between those sheets with her.

"No, I really do."

"Oh, okay." Her face falls and she climbs into bed while I make a makeshift sleeping area next to the bed.

There's no way I'm going to survive this trip without falling head over heels for her.

paula

I CAN'T FREAKING SLEEP. Especially not knowing Tristan is sleeping on the cold ass floor. A part of me wants to wake him up and tell him to get in the bed. But I know he won't. He made that abundantly clear before I tried, unsuccessfully, to fall asleep.

He really is sweet to take the floor and not make me uncomfortable. But I'm perfectly capable of sleeping with someone without *sleeping* with them. Though, it'd be really nice to cuddle with anybody. The house is freezing, and this blanket isn't doing its job. If Mom would leave the damn heater alone, I would be nice and toasty.

He rolls over, and I swear I see his eyes slam shut when he sees me. Is he having a hard time falling asleep, too?

"Tristan," I whisper.

He doesn't budge. Maybe I imagined it.

"Tristan, are you awake?" My voice is slightly louder this time.

Nothing. I know I saw his eyes open.

"Tristan. Are you sleeping?" My voice is louder still.

Hopefully I won't wake anyone else up. My mom has a really good ear, especially on family vacations, since we used to try to sneak out to go night swimming.

"I'm trying to." He finally responds. His voice is deep and gravelly, completely unlike the way he normally talks. It's probably not a good sign the sound sends a shiver through my body. And now I feel bad I probably woke him up for no reason.

He turns toward me. "What do you need?"

Even now, he's a sweetheart. If the tables were turned, I can't say I'd be so gracious.

Crap. I just wanted to see if he was awake.

"Are you, um, cold?"

"A little bit, but I'll be fine."

First order of business when we all wake up is to go out and buy bigger blankets. The ones supplied by the house are comfortable, but they are meant for the summer months. I'm sure they don't have a ton of people who rent beach houses in the winter. Well, except for my parents.

"You can get up here with me if you'd like."

A groan sounds in his throat. "I really can't, Paula."

Is there something so grotesque about me that he doesn't want to be in the same space as me? But he let me cuddle with him on the sofa, so I don't think it's that. And the kiss we shared in the parking lot was pretty up close and personal.

"You know I don't bite, right?" So, what if my words are dripping in sarcasm.

"I know." He sighs. "But in order for me to play my role in this facade, I need to set some boundaries for myself."

Oh. That thought never crossed my mind. Maybe it should have. "I understand."

"Thank you. If things were different...." His words hang in the air as he rolls back over. I know how that sentence ends and a small part of me wishes I would have asked him to be here with me for real.

"Hi, Big Sis." Piper's voice scares the shit out of me and I fall off the bed.

It takes me a few moments to remember Tristan was lying on the floor beneath me. I scramble backwards and realize he isn't there. How long has he been up?

"Don't worry about your *boyfriend*. He's in the kitchen with Mom and Dad, having coffee."

Oh, thank God. He didn't run for the hills. Not that he could since we came in my car. There are ways he could get back home if he wanted to. "Why are you in my bed? And being creepy?"

Her grin is unsettling, and dread forms in the pit of my stomach. "I have a better question. Why is your boyfriend sleeping on the floor? Unless, of course, he's not really your boyfriend."

Damn her, and how perceptive she is. But I can totally play this off. There are plenty of reasons. "Don't be ridiculous. We are definitely dating."

"That would be a good band name." She cocks her head to the side. "But that doesn't answer the question."

"Why is my word not enough?"

"Because, Paula, this is weird behavior, even for you." She sits up and crisscrosses her legs in front of her. "You've never really been one to flaunt your personal life in front of anyone. And just because you don't talk to the big bad brother and parents, doesn't mean you don't talk to the rest of us. Me and Parker know something is up. You've never once mentioned Tristan to either of us."

"Maybe if y'all would text me back, I would have told y'all." She has to realize it's a two-way street, whether she wants to or not.

"I feel like if you had a boyfriend, and wanted us more awesome siblings to know, you would have sent the first text. Don't put the blame on us because you're trying to hide something."

I can't let her keep thinking this thing is fake. While I don't think she would intentionally spill the beans, it would slip out. It always does.

"Look, he slept on the floor because he didn't want to be disrespectful to Mom and Dad. He's old-fashioned like that."

There. A totally plausible reason he would be sleeping on the floor. I only hope she buys it.

She eyes me wearily, but seems to accept that answer. "I'll be watching the two of you. Parker, too."

I grab Tristan's pillow and throw it at her, missing her completely. "You sound like a villain."

Smirking, she grabs the pillow and chunks back at me. It hits me in the face despite turning away. She's like a freaking magician.

"I never claimed to be anything but one." She climbs off the bed and heads toward the door. "Mom is cooking soon. If you want to get to your boy toy before our brother's do, I'd get in there now."

'Ugh, fine. I'm coming."

As soon as she closes the door behind her. I get off the floor. My legs have goosebumps and I don't understand how Tristan slept comfortably down here. Hopefully I can talk some sense into him tonight.

I grab his blankets off the floor and toss them on the bed before folding them. I don't want Mom coming in here and finding the mess on the floor. That's not something she would get too mad about. But I don't want to answer any questions she might have. Piper and her are a lot alike in that respect. They won't let anything go if they don't like the answer.

I grab an oversized sweatshirt I threw on the dresser last night and slip it over my head. It completely covers my shorts. Maybe I should put on some leggings instead. Nope. I'm not going to do it. Mom and Dad are used to seeing me like this after bed. If I'm going to prove that me and Tristan are a thing to my youngest siblings, they have to see I'm comfortable being in front of him in every capacity.

Okay, I can totally do this. I may not have any theatre

experience, but I've always been a fake it until you make it type of girl. It's how I landed the job at Whoopsie Daisy. I didn't know anything about flowers until my first day there. Now, I'm learning how to make arrangements.

Cracking open the bedroom door, I listen for any noise outside of the voices drifting from the kitchen. It seems like my other siblings are still asleep. Thank God for small mercies.

My steps are soft as I slip out of the room and gently close the door behind me. As much as I'd like my presence known, I want to know what Tristan and my parents are talking about. Nosiness seems to be a trait all of us Summers' kids seem to have.

"Have you tried our wine?" Dad asks. He's loud by nature and it's a shock nobody else has woken up from his booming voice. "I have some here. You should try it."

"Paul." Mom admonishes him. "It's way too early for wine. The poor boy hasn't even eaten yet."

"A little wine before breakfast is fine." A bottle slides across the table before sliding back. Mom probably gave him one of her famous looks. "Maybe after dinner instead."

"I actually tried some at Out of the Ashes one night. I think Paula told me it was a sangria. It was really good."

Dad chuckles. "It's probably one of our most popular bottles."

"I can see why." Tristan replies.

Well, it appears he's won over the parents. That's a

miracle. I figured they'd dislike him on sight because I didn't tell anyone about him.

Okay, time to stop eavesdropping. I can definitely use some coffee after tossing and turning last night from being cold.

I make my steps louder so they won't realize I was listening in. When I come around the corner, Tristan chokes as soon as he sees me. He'll have to get better about acting natural to me being in my jammies. Otherwise, they'll never buy we've been together for a bit.

"Is everything okay, Tristan?" Mom asks as she pulls a carton of eggs out of the fridge.

"Yes, ma'am. Went down the wrong pipe is all."

"How many times do I have to tell you? Call me Abigail, please." She catches sight of me. "Good morning, sweetheart. There's coffee in the pot."

"Thanks, Mom." I move around her to get to the coffee pot. There are a row of mugs already lined up on the counter. Six of them which means Piper hasn't made her appearance in here yet. I wonder why she's waiting.

After I pour a cup, I add some sugar, and ask Mom for the creamer. Now that I've got my coffee the way I like it, I lift the cup and let the warmth take away the cold in my hands.

Tristan's eyes are still on me as I make my way to the table. I place a quick kiss on top of his head before sitting on the bench beside him. "Morning."

"Morning." He bumps into me. "I hope I didn't wake you when I got out of bed."

Ah, so he *is* making it seem like we were in the same bed.

"Nope. My sister did the honors." His eyes widen for a split second before he regains control. "She decided to scare the hell out of me."

"Language while at the table, Paula," Mom says without a glance backward.

"Fine." I grumble. "How long have you been up?"

"About thirty minutes." Tristan shrugs. "Your parents were already in here when I came in. Honestly, I think it's the smell of coffee that pulled me out of my slumber."

"Speaking of sleep." I change the subject. "Are there extra blankets? The room was freezing last night."

"Your brothers took whatever extra blankets were available." Mom is scrambling eggs while flipping bacon. I, on the other hand, can barely boil water while talking. "Sorry about turning the heat down. Menopause has me all over the place."

Okay, that may have been too much information in front of a guest, but I am choosing my battles wisely this morning.

"Well, I guess I'm going to the store after breakfast." Mom turns around as if I've somehow wounded her. "Nothing against you, Mom." I hold my hands up in surrender. "I don't want you to make yourself uncomfortable on account of me. I'll buy a comforter that matches my room so I'll get more than a couple of uses from it."

"That's smart, kiddo." Dad adds. As if he won't be

doing everything in his power to get me to work for the winery later.

"While you're out, can you get some things. It was a mistake asking your brothers to do any sort of shopping. I know you'll get what I need."

"Sure thing." I guess being an eldest daughter never fades. I'm always there to help in any way I can, and it's one of the reasons they think they can push me into a position.

tristan

"YOUR FAMILY DOESN'T SEEM SO bad." We're at the store looking for a blanket, along with the massive list of stuff Abigail asked us to get. It's like she's feeding a basketball team. Which, I guess, she is with how many people are in the family. There were only three of us home most of the time unless my brother came home to visit.

"That's what you think. Just wait until we start playing games. Or, even worse, my brother starts needling me about taking on my family obligations."

She's leaning over the cart as she pushes it toward the home goods area. The good thing about chain stores is almost all of them look the same so we aren't spending a ton of time looking for things. But Paula has been here many times, it makes sense she knows the store well.

"Oh, you also need to sleep in the bed with me."

Whoa, that came out of nowhere. She also picks up her speed as if the conversation is over now that she's said her piece. It's not that I don't want to sleep next to her. But I don't know that I can keep my emotions out of it. Eric was right. This is a lot harder than I thought it would be. I was trying to be nice, but keeping my feelings locked away in a box is proving to be difficult.

"Why?" I lengthen my strides to catch up with her. "I thought we agreed on this arrangement before we came down here."

She nods her acknowledgment. "That was before my sister paid me a visit this morning and noticed your bedding on the floor. Both her and Parker are onto us. She said they'll be keeping an eye on us the entire time."

This is what she meant about her siblings meddling all the time. A small part of me is grateful I never had to deal with that. I would have lost my mind. Even my parents never meddled in my life, but we also shared what was going on freely.

"Would it be so bad if they knew? Out of all your siblings they seem like the coolest."

"Oh, I'm closer to them than I am any of the others. But that's part of the problem." She pauses so another person can come out of the aisle we need to enter.

"How?" If she's close to them, they'll understand.

"Because I've never mentioned you. That's red flag number one. And, as much as I love my sister, she cannot keep a secret for shit. She doesn't do it on purpose, but whatever she's trying to hide always slips out. That's how I got in trouble most of the time in my teens. It would be weeks after I did something and she'd say something in passing. Then I'd be grounded or have to do extra chores."

"Oh. And what about Parker?"

She stops in front of the row of comforters, studying each one. To my surprise she bypasses all the neutral colored ones, and heads straight for the bright, bold colors. I don't know why I'm shocked. Talking to her these past couple of weeks, I've noticed she's not quite as subdued as she wants people to believe. She stands out in a crowd. Though, that may be because I really like her.

I also appreciate her trying to protect me from her family, but I can handle myself. She needs to give me the opportunity to show her.

"Parker is like a vault for the most part. But I wouldn't put it past him to poke holes in everything we say. Like I said last night, he's the biggest prankster I know. It's like being a pain in the ass gives him strength."

Ah. That actually makes sense and fits the vibe he gave off last night. It looks like my studying didn't matter. Her siblings are all completely different than I thought they would be. And here I thought I'd actually be more friendly to her older brother. That one may take some work on my part. I will win him over before we leave.

"So, what you're saying is we need to be absolutely ridiculous."

She glances from the comforter in her hands to me. "Yes, but also, I'm not sure what you mean by that."

"More PDA, sleeping in the same bed." I pause and tap my fingers on the edge of the cart. "Should we come up with nicknames for each other? You know like those couples in cheesy movies?"

"Absolutely fucking not." She glares at me. "If you call me something other than Paula, or babe, I won't be responsible for how I respond."

"So, no puddin' pop." I don't know where I even pulled the name from but the disgust on her face is worth the suggestion.

"You really want me to get kicked out of this store, don't you?"

"I'm kidding. Sort of." I hold my hands up in surrender.

"Keep pressing buttons, buddy. I'll tell Parker you're fair game." She looks at the bright pink comforter in her hands to another one the shelf. It's turquoise and seems to have a floral print on in it. "I don't know which one to get."

Grabbing the one from her hands I set it in the basket. Then I reach up and pull the one from the shelf before tossing it beside the first. "We'll get both."

"I only need one, though."

"The way you were acting last night, you'll probably need both before the weekend is over."

"But I—"

"No, buts. I'm getting both of them for you. Now, let's tackle this list your mom made. How many days does she think we're staying?"

Instead of arguing with me over the comforter, she grabs the list out of my hand. At least I seem to have won this round.

"Do you remember how much you ate as a teenager?"

"Not much has changed between then and now."

"Multiply that by six, then add in you and my dad."

"Yeah, this makes a bit more sense."

"I'll be surprised if there's any of the junk food they bought last night left by the end of the day."

"You should give them a bit more credit than that." I know her siblings don't make things too easy for her, but they deserve some slack. The only thing I can do is give them a chance. I'll let them prove themselves to me on their own.

"Eh, you didn't grow up with them."

"Touché." She has an experience I've never had. I mean the entire crew of Crooked Halo are like family, but it's not the same as growing up with them. We're all adults. This is one I area I wish I could connect with her. That will never happen, though. Now to figure out how I'm going to sleep in the same bed with her.

It took everyone to bring the groceries in earlier. For such a small kitchen, it holds all the food with ease. There's not a stray item on the counters. It's also a good thing I didn't make a bet with Paula earlier. Phillip just popped the last pizza pocket in the microwave.

"What are you doing?" Abigail yells as soon as she hears the electronic hum.

"Eating a snack." Phillip sounds confused by the question.

"We're going to eat in a bit. You'll ruin your appetite." She admonishes.

He shrinks back a bit before busting out in laughter. "You know I'll be hungry again in thirty minutes. You don't have to worry about me not wanting to eat."

She rolls her eyes and turns toward the hallway. I guess even she needs a break from her kids on occasion.

Phillip grabs his food from the microwave and doesn't wait for it to cool down before taking a huge bite. He's doing that awkward thing where you chew and try to keep from burning the inside of your mouth. I don't think I've ever seen anyone actually do it. It's quite funny.

After he swallows, he leans against the counter. "How did you and Paula meet?"

The sibling inquisition took longer than I thought it would. They didn't really get a chance this morning, though. Paula and I left before they made it to the kitchen.

"Yeah, how did y'all meet? My sister never said." Pierce pipes in from the living room. Damn this open floor plan. I really hoped he wasn't listening in. Though he is the one I have to win over.

Remember to stick as close to the truth as possible.

"We met at Out of the Ashes."

"Figures." Pierce rolls his eyes.

"The story has to be better than that."

"Well, I bumped into her and her phone flew out of her hand. I gave it back to her, we had drinks, and the rest is history. I'm on the road a lot so we hang out when I'm in town."

It's not a complete lie. I am on the road a lot.

"So, you drive trucks or something?" Pierce's tone is condescending at best. I don't understand why he has it out for me when he doesn't even know me. Maybe Paula is right and he can't be brought to my side.

"Absolutely not. There isn't anything wrong with it, I just don't do that. I'm actually part of the crew for a band."

"What band?" Phillip throws his trash away and moves closer to me. Personal space isn't a thing with this family. Got it.

"Crooked Halo."

"Oh my God. No way." Phillip's smile is wide and excited. "I try to see them every time they are in town. I've seen them once when they are on tour, but I like when they play at Out of the Ashes. It feels more…"

"Intimate?" I add to help him out.

"Exactly." He is staring at me in awe. "It must be so cool working with them. I never get a chance to talk to them after a set because they are surrounded by people."

Do I tell him they are making Asheville home base? I'm not sure they want that to be public information. I'll keep my mouth shut for now.

"Text me next time you're there to see them play. I'll make sure you get a chance to meet them. Dale tries to make time to meet everyone, but it can be hard sometimes."

"That would be so awesome. I'll make sure you have my number by the end of the weekend."

I glance over my shoulder at Pierce and see a scowl across his face. He doesn't seem happy his little brother likes me. Well, he likes my job, but still. I'll take a win however I get it.

"So, I hear you do actually use your phone." Pierce says to someone behind me.

It's Paula, I know it is. As wild as it sounds, I could feel her presence as soon as she came into the room.

"I don't know who told you that. I despise that thing." She's grinning when I turn toward her. Making jokes is how she tries to change the subject, and I hate she has do it with her own family.

"Tristan said he saved it after knocking it out of your hands at the bar." He glances between us to see if I lied. "I didn't think it worked seeing as how you never answer when I call."

"That's because I don't answer people I don't want to talk to."

"Well, thanks for that."

Phillip looks between the three of us. "You answer me."

"Not helping," she mutters.

"Are you kidding me?" Pierce stands. "Am I the only sibling you won't respond to?"

She shrugs. "I don't answer for Peter most of the time either."

"That's just great." He throws his hands in the air

and comes around the couch. "You need to grow up and take on your family responsibilities."

"And that right there is why I don't answer your calls." She points her finger at him. "It's never a call to see how I'm doing or what I've been up to. It's always when are you going to stop fucking around and work at the winery."

"It's your du—"

Before he has a chance to finish, she rushes past me and her brothers. The door opens and slams behind her.

My first instinct is to follow after her. Instead, I turn toward Pierce. "I don't know what your problem is, and I clearly don't know your family dynamic, but that doesn't give you the right to order her around or tell her what to do. She is your sister, and a whole ass human being. You won't speak to her like that again."

Without giving him a chance to respond, I rush to the room and grab a jacket before hauling ass out the front door. Paula and I may not be a real couple, but I'll be damned if her family goes out of her way to make her feel like shit.

paula

IT DIDN'T EVEN TAKE a full twenty-four hours for my brother to lay into me. How did an innocent conversation take such a hard left turn?

Pierce didn't say anything after Tristan said how we met, which he did perfectly. I was listening from the hallway. Creepy? Maybe. Do I care? No.

I thought all crappy comments from my older brother would be held back after Phillip geeked out over Tristan working for Crooked Halo. But no. He waited until I came into the room to lay into me. The only thing I did was walk into the room.

The sand shifts beneath my feet, and slips into my shoes as I stomp across the beach. It's not giving me the angry satisfaction I so desperately want. The sand is too soft to get that frustrated sound I'm looking for.

I'm not sure how far I am from the house. I didn't think when I stormed out. The only thing fueling me was the need to get out of there and away from Pierce.

Loathing bubbles up to the surface. He always has to do something other than make my life hell. Even growing up, he would do whatever he could to catch me doing something I wasn't supposed to all to get me in trouble. Never the other siblings. Just me.

Honestly, it feels like he's had it out for me since day one. Siblings are supposed to get along, not make each other feel like shit. I've watched the relationship between Kai and Kate. While they bicker, it's all in good fun. They don't go out of their way to intentionally make the other feel like crap. I have that with most of brothers and sister. The only ones I've never meshed well with are Pierce and Peter. As much as I'd like to change that, I'm not sure it ever will.

If I don't focus on something else, I'll end up packing my bags and leaving. Even though I didn't want to be here to begin with, I don't want to leave in anger.

The beach is secluded. Not a single person as far as I can see. Probably because they are smart. It's cooler by the water than I thought it would be. That's what I get for acting out of frustration, but being cold out here is better than fighting with my brother.

Breathe, Paula. Breathe.

The waves crashing against the shore is the soundtrack to my breathe exercise. I breathe the salty air in and out. My pounding heartbeat begins to slow and even out. I'm no longer trying to stomp my anger out. It's still there, but not all consuming the way it was minutes ago.

Maybe Emily is rubbing off on me more than she thought. I've watched her go over mediation techniques with Samantha countless times. Even Kate needs her help at times to cool off when a bride is being overly dramatic.

It's a good thing I found these ladies when I did. Otherwise, there's a possibility I would have gotten into an actual fight with my brother. Not that he'd lay a hand on me, but I don't know if I would forgive myself if I lashed out like that.

Running and hiding seems like a much more viable way to handle things. The sun is setting and I need to head back, but I can't bring myself to turn around. I wrap my arms tighter around myself to try to stave off the cold.

I feel something wrap around my shoulders and I turn too fast. My balance is gone, but I don't hit the sand.

Arms wrap around me and I'm staring up at Tristan. "This time you tried to kill me."

"Sorry about that." His soft chuckle is everything I need right now. A friendly face to push away all the crap with my brother. "I tried calling your name, but I don't think you heard me."

"How long have you been following me?"

"Not long." He helps me stand and adjusts the jacket he put over my shoulders. "I came after you, but you seemed like you needed some time, so I hung back."

"Oh." The fact he can read me better than my family is an oddity. We've been around each other a handful of times, but he seems to know me better than most despite every wall I've put up against him. "Thank you for the jacket."

"No problem." He shrugs and shoves his hands in his pockets. His thin, long sleeved shirt isn't going to do much against the cold, and I feel bad he gave me his only source of warmth. "You didn't take anything with you, and I thought you might get cold. Looks like I was right."

Neither of us says another word. The ocean waves are the only soundtrack, and it feels easy. Like this is how it's supposed to be. He doesn't try to rush me back to the house. Only stands in solidarity until I decide what *I* want to do.

His phone dings in his pocket, but he doesn't rush to pull it out. His sole focus is on me.

"Are you gonna get that?"

"It can wait."

It dings two more times.

"You should probably see who that is."

He shakes his head, but pulls his phone out and glances at the screen. His eyebrows pinch in confusion.

"How did he get my number?"

"Who?"

"Parker. He said they're about to leave for dinner and we should hurry back."

"I'm going to kill him."

Tristan taps out a quick response and pockets his phone again.

"Why?"

"Because the little jerk went through my contacts. And if he saw our text messages, then he *knows* we aren't actually dating. He better keep his mouth shut." Nothing about the past few minutes feels fake, though.

"That's a future problem." He waits for me to say something else, but I don't. What else is there to say? "I told him to send me the address and we'll meet them there."

"We should probably head back." I don't want to burst this bubble of calm I have, but I know if we don't meet up with the family, I'll have to answer to my parents. Shockingly they weren't the cause of this afternoon's explosion.

"Whenever you're ready. We go on your time, not theirs." He slides his hand into mine. "I'm by your side, you don't have to worry."

Every part of me melts at the words. Not once has anyone put me, and my wants, first. It's always what I can do for them.

"Sorry about earlier." My focus is on the sand ahead of us as I lead us back to the beach house. I'm not even sure how far away we are.

"You don't need to apologize. You didn't do anything wrong." He gives my hand a quick squeeze. "What's his problem anyway?"

"Honestly, I have no idea. There's always been friction between us for as long as I can remember. Part of me wonders if he's mad because he's not Dad's namesake. Or if he never wanted a little sister. It's just weird because he's not like this with the other siblings."

Tristan is quiet for a moment, letting what I've said sink in. It's one of the things I'm coming to admire about him. He doesn't fly off the handle like me. He takes time to consider what he wants to say.

"Do you think it's because you don't fall in line with the rest of your siblings? From the outside looking in, it seems like he's trying to be a parent instead of a brother. That isn't fair to you, or him."

I never thought of it like that. Looking back, he has always put himself in that role. I don't understand why. Our parents have always been around and did their job. They still do.

"It's probably because Dad is preparing him to take over the company. He's been getting him ready for it for as long as I can remember. He knows it's part of our family legacy, and I think me not wanting to do it is a thorn in his side."

"That could be it. But there's no reason for him to be a jackass about the situation. Each person is allowed to do what they want. Working for the winery isn't something you want to do right now, and he shouldn't pressure you into it."

He's not wrong, but he also hasn't had something like this held over his head his entire life. Despite all the stuff with the winery, we're a closeknit family. Even though I don't really talk to Pierce on a personal level, he knows what's going on in my life. All of our siblings talk, and we hang out. He's never pushed as hard as he is now, though. That's the problem.

"I'll figure out a way to talk to him about while we're here. I can't make any promises, but I'll try."

He pulls us to stop and moves in front of me. Lifting his free hand to my face, he tilts my head until my eyes meet his.

"Wrong answer. Remember that deal we made for me to come with you? You have to stand up for yourself. I'll be right beside you if you need me to be, but you can do it."

Shit. I forgot about that little stipulation. We still have three more days of this trip. That's plenty of time to take my stand. Maybe.

"Okay."

"That's it? Okay? You're not going to fight me on this?" He seems confused.

"It's been a long afternoon. I'm afraid I don't have any fight left at the moment." I'm not lying. Even though the spat with Pierce was brief, it took a lot out of me. Maybe it's because it happened in front of Tristan. I don't know. But I don't have it in me to put up another argument right now.

"I guess it's a good thing you have me here to help you do just that when the time comes."

"That means more than you realize." Everything he's done in the twenty-four hours we've been here has been to make sure I'm okay and comfortable. He really doesn't know how much it means that someone is putting me first.

"Oh, I think I do." He leans closer.

Is he about to kiss me? I've been looking forward to this part of our performance since our practice kiss in the parking lot.

Except right now we don't have an audience. This is something he *wants* to do. I move to meet him, and my stomach decides it's a perfect time to growl.

Tristan chuckles and pulls away. "We should probably hurry so we can get you fed."

Damn you stomach. For a split second he looked at me like more than a friend, and maybe that's something I want. Ugh, stupid feelings. This is why I've never done relationships. These emotions are confusing.

tristan

THE DRIVE to the restaurant is quiet. Paula is staring out the window as I follow the map on the screen. We've left the beach front and are going further into town.

I think I may have overstepped in my thoughts on her brother. Or maybe it was me leaning into to kiss her. I probably shouldn't have done that. But...she leaned in, too. She obviously feels some sort of way about me. I hope by the end of the trip, I'll know where we stand. If she wants to stay friends, I'm cool with it. Paula is fun to hang out with, and she doesn't filter her words or thoughts.

We're getting closer to our destination, but I don't see anything signaling we're going to a restaurant.

"Are we in the right place?" The question feels loud in the silence. Like I've interrupted the serenity of the space.

"Huh?" She turns toward me, and I'm taken aback by her beauty in the dim dashboard lights. Relaxed is the only way I can describe her right now. After her argument with Pierce and the walk on the beach, she seems like she's at peace. At least, for now.

"Is the area we're supposed to be in? It looks like it's just a bunch of houses."

"Oh, yeah." She points ahead of us. "Find the first parking spot you can. It's hard to find close parking, even during off season."

"Sure thing." I've been to some hole in the wall restaurants in my time with Crooked Halo, but this really looks like a residential area.

Someone is pulling out of a parking space, and I wait to pull in. I'm not taking any chances even if I don't know where I'm at. Before Paula has a chance to open her door, I turn off the car and rush around to her side. It's the little things. Not only is it part of the dating thing, but I was raised to be a gentleman. My dad still opens the door for my mom and they've been together for decades. It's sweet.

"Thank you," she says as I offer my hand to help her out.

"Any time." I pull her closer to me and wrap an arm around her waist. It's still pretty chilly, and she took my jacket off when we got back to the beach house.

"Is this place good?" I've never heard of it, and I don't know what to expect.

"Definitely." She nods. "They serve a little bit of everything and the food is delicious. They even have fountain *Big Red*, and that's probably my favorite thing."

"That's good to know." I give her a quick squeeze.

"Sounds like an easy way to get back into your good graces when I screw up."

"Are you talking about while we're here? Or, when we go back to the real world and we're just friends."

The acknowledgment of our expiration dates hits me right in the heart. I know it's not her casting me out of her life forever. But the more time I spend with her, I don't know that I'll ever be able to *only* be friends with her again.

"Both." I force a small laugh to hide the pain.

We've come to small building on the corner, and I can only assume this is the right place. A blast of hot air hits me as soon as I pull the door open. There's a line along the wall of people waiting to order. Wow, this place must be popular.

The room we're in has tables sprinkled through, and none of them are empty. Paula's family is also nowhere to be seen.

"Do you think they went to another restaurant?" I don't want to take up space in here if we need to leave.

"No, there's another dining area off to the side." Paula assures me. She pulls out her phone from her small purse and sends a text. It dings with a response right away. "Piper said they've saved us some seats. And, they are far away from Pierce."

That feels like an added bonus for her. We definitely don't need to rehash earlier events in a public space. Though, I'm sure her brother knows that.

We're slowly making progress to the front of the line, and I start perusing the lit-up menu behind the counter.

"So, what's good here?" I haven't had much seafood. The band prefers Mexican food, and we always try to find hidden gems to eat at.

"Pretty much anything." She waves toward the menu. "If you don't like seafood, they have burgers and chicken strips. Though I definitely recommend the grilled shrimp. They make it to perfection."

"Okay, then. That's what I'm getting."

"You don't have to get the same thing as me. Or, eat seafood for that matter."

"Paula, I value your opinion. I've never really eaten seafood before. Is life even worth living if you don't try new things?"

She flinches at the question, and I want to know why. I won't push her, though. She'll tell me or she won't. That's up to her.

"Okay, but don't blame me when you learn you love it, and will want it all the time." She smirks pushing aside whatever concerned her only seconds ago.

We place our order, and I pay for it despite her protests. She better get used to it. As long as I'm around, I'll take care of things. Fake boyfriend or not.

"Do we wait here for the food?"

"Nope. That's what this is for." She holds up a small plastic tent with a number on it. "Let's go find my family, and hope some of them are in better moods." The last thing is said just above a whisper.

I follow her through a door on the side of the room. It leads outside to a pathway. There's another door on the other side, and laughter can be heard before we open it.

Her family is on the far side of the room, taking up almost half of it. I wonder why this place doesn't look for a bigger location. It's popular enough to afford it. Maybe the cozy vibe is part of the appeal. It feels like a big family get together. At least, it does, based on what I've seen in movies. I wouldn't know from personal experience.

"You finally made it." Paul stands shakes my hand. It's not like we didn't see each other earlier, or are staying under the same room for a few days. Formalities must be a big thing for him.

"Yes, sir. Sorry we're late."

"It's fine. Take a seat." He holds his hands toward the two open seats by Parker and Piper. Apparently, everyone knew Paula would need to be around friendly faces tonight.

Pierce doesn't acknowledge us. He's either still mad about his sister intentionally ignoring him, or at me for scolding him. I have a feeling that doesn't happen to him too often.

"How was your walk on the beach?" Parker leans in front of me to ask his sister.

"It was fine." Paula huffs. "But don't think we won't be talking about you going through my phone later."

"I don't know what you're talking about." He gasps and puts his hand over his heart.

At the same time Piper says, "I thought I was the only one who did that."

"What?" Paula's head snaps to her sister.

I don't know what I would do with this sort of invasion of privacy. There truly are no secrets in this family. Well, except that I'm not really Paula's boyfriend. Hell, I'm barely a friend.

"It might be time to put a passcode on your phone." I chuckle and bump into Paula.

"Won't help." Piper sighs. "I would figure it out."

"Or lock me out of my phone." Paula grumbles. She glances at her siblings. "Why haven't you eaten? Your food is getting cold."

"We were waiting for you." Parker says as he grabs a fry and pops it in his mouth. "We couldn't let you eat alone."

"What am I? Chopped liver?" It's like all of them forgot I even exist.

"No." Piper laughs. "But since you're together, you're counted as one unit. I don't make the rules."

Not going to lie, I like the way it sounds being one unit with Paula. If I push too hard, she'll shut me down faster than I can get the words out of my mouth. I'd rather not show my hand before I know where she stands. There are moments like now when she leans into me while talking with her family that I think there may be something there. That I'm not the only one who feels the sparks between us. Time will tell, and I'm not willing to rush it.

Our food arrives and we chat with everyone while eating. Phillip is peppering me with questions about Crooked Halo. He might be their biggest fan. I have to make a meeting happen between him and Dale. Even

Peter is joining in the conversation. Maybe he's softening up toward me.

Pierce, however, keeps most of his attention on his parents. I can't figure out what they are talking about since he's on the opposite end of the table. It looks serious, though. Hopefully Paula isn't the topic because I'll step in if she needs me to. I'm not scared to go to bat for her.

We finish up our conversations, and the restaurant is clearing out. I'm not even sure how long we've been here. The food has been long gone, but the time has been enjoyable.

This time with all the siblings in one spot has let me learn a bit more about them. Piper and Parker are more laid-back versions of Paula. Phillip goes with the flow and isn't bothered by much. Peter is more like Pierce, but he seems more approachable, less hardened by life.

Pierce, I'm sure someone could write a dissertation on the chip is has on his shoulder. He's very serious, and I don't think I've seen him crack a smile once. I hope whatever his problem is, he drops it in regards to Paula.

"Are we ready to head home?" Abigail allows Paul to help her slide on her jacket before grabbing her purse. "I'm pretty sure they are closing soon, and we're the last ones here."

"Actually," Piper says. "I think I may head to the bar by the beach and have a few drinks. Anyone want to join me?"

Parker raises his hands as if he's a student waiting to

be called on. Even Phillip and Peter add their hands to the mix.

I lean over and whisper, "We'll do whatever you want. We can go out with your siblings, or head back to the beach house."

Piper seems to sense her sister's indecision, and asks, "What about you big brother. You gonna come hang out with the rest of the brood?"

"I think I'm going to call it a night. We have to get up early to check out a winery."

"Oh, well have fun with that." She waves.

"All of us are going." He gives Paula a pointed look. She simply nods in response.

"So, what do you want to do?" I ask again.

"Screw it. Let's go out. You only live once, right?" She grabs her purse from the back of the chair.

There she is. The girl I first saw at Out of the Ashes. Tomorrow morning is going to suck, but it'll be worth it.

CHAPTER THIRTEEN

GOING out with my siblings was a bad idea. No, scratch that, a terrible idea. I'm going to feel this in the morning. All six of us are doing our best to tiptoe into the house. Peter slips and crashes into the table.

"Be quiet," I hiss. "Do you want to wake up Mom and Dad? Or, even worse, Pierce?"

"Oh God." Peter groans. "I'd rather wake up our parents than him."

Huh, at least he realizes the absolute terror our big brother can be. I always thought he had some sort of hero worship happening where he was concerned. I guess you learn something new every day.

You'd think with all of us growing up with a winery, we'd have a high tolerance for alcohol. It's not the case, at all.

Me, Piper, and Parker are mostly fine. Tristan didn't drink so he could drive us all home. He's too sweet for his own good. Peter and Phillip on the other hand...there is no way they will feel up to going to check out the winery.

Tristan turns to me and pulls me to a stop. "You wait right here. I'm going to make sure the rest of them get to their beds."

I mock salute him and sit on the sofa. Tonight was more fun that I thought it would be. If Pierce had gone, he would have been a bump on the log and made everyone else miserable. I'm happy he decided to come home.

I think back to earlier in the night when Tristan asked me to dance. It's not something I normally do, but I wanted to with him. That was before I even finished my first drink. His hands on my hips as we moved to the rhythm of the music, and it felt good. Better than I've felt with anyone else. Each and every moment I spend with him, changes the dynamics between us.

My sister would say alcohol has something to do with it all the emotions, but even now I'm not drunk. I know how to have a good time without getting shit faced, unlike my siblings.

The absolute joy I'm sitting with is from spending time with my family without having to worry about any obligations. Hell, nobody even brought it up. Why can't our eldest brother do the same thing?

"Why are you brothers so hard to put to bed? I swear they are like babies." Tristan whispers as he comes back into the living room.

"That's how they've always been. I can't tell you the number of times I've had to cover for them." Maybe that's why Pierce doesn't like me. I was there for the younger ones the way he should have been there for me.

"I believe it." He reaches for my hand and I let him take it. "Are you ready for bed?"

"Oh my gosh, yes. It's been a long freaking day. And I hear my new comforter calling me."

He doesn't say anything else, only leads me into our room. My new pink comforter is spread across the bed and it clashes with everything in this room, but I don't even care. At least I know I'll be warm tonight.

"I'm gonna go change in the restroom so you can get your jammies on."

"You don't have to." I try to argue but he holds up his hand.

"I really do." He grabs some things out of his bag. "I'll be right back."

Tristan runs hot and cold. At times I know he feels something toward me, and then he plays the perfect gentleman. I don't know if it's for my benefit or his. But I can't help wondering. We've only been *together* for a day, but we've been talking for a couple of weeks, and I've gotten to know him a bit better through that time. We mesh well together.

I knew doing a fake relationship was going to be a bad idea. It's hard not to develop feelings for someone you're friendly with. Deep down I know, that's starting to happen. I've never had an inkling of more than surface level attraction with anyone else. There's something different with Tristan, though. Something I didn't realize I want in my life.

Quickly, I grab my pajamas out of the dresser and change. Next time we do a trip like this, I need to remember to bring sweats. My shorts are not cutting it with how cold the house is.

I slide beneath the comforter just as Tristan opens the bedroom door. "Are you good?"

"Yep. All changed and ready for bed." Now I wait to see what he does.

He walks around the bed and picks up the bedding he used last night. Damn, I guess he's not going to sleep in the bed with me. It's like he wants the two youngest to find us out, even though I'm sure they already know.

To my surprise, he goes back to the other side of the bed. What is he doing? But I hold off on saying anything. Curiosity is getting the best of me.

He sets the blanket on the end of the bed before lining up the pillow down the middle. I can't help it, I have to ask, "What are you doing?"

"Getting the bed ready to sleep with you." He cocks his head to the side as if it should be obvious.

"Why are you putting the pillows between us?"

"If there's something between us, there won't be any temptation to take things further. You don't cross the pillow line, and I won't either."

I start laughing and immediately cover my mouth. I do not want Parker or Piper walking in on this.

"If that's what makes you feel better, I guess."

"It does." After he's done building a barrier between us, he lifts the comforter and slides onto the bed. "Good night, Paula."

With those parting words, he turns off the lamp and rolls over. Oh, so I guess he has to be facing away from me as well. This does answer my earlier musings about if he's attracted to me. He obviously is if he has to put an obstacle between us. I just wish he'd let himself act on it.

Normally, I can turn over and go straight to sleep. Having someone beside me in the bed has never been a problem since I've been sharing beds with my siblings my entire life.

But tonight, that isn't happening. Even though Tristan breathing has evened out, I know he's not asleep. He keeps tossing, turning, and pulling the covers tighter over him to strengthen the shield he's built.

He also makes a lot of noise when he moves. It's so loud I'm surprised the entire house can't hear him.

I'm not sure how long I lay there, but I can't take it anymore. I grab each pillow, one by one and throw them on the floor.

This time he turns toward me. "What are you doing?"

"Getting rid of these damn pillows. They're annoying."

"But I put them there for a reason." He sounds frustrated, but not mad. Which is a good thing, because I don't care if he's mad.

"It's a dumb reason. We are both grown adults and are capable of sleeping in the bed together. Besides with the pillows there, I can't do this."

I walk my fingers across his side before scooting closer to him, testing his boundaries.

"Paula, this isn't a good idea."

"Says who?"

"Me," he sighs. "You've been drinking. And I can't be intimate with somebody who doesn't feel the same way I do." I'm surprised he isn't ticking the reasons off on his fingers.

I knew that going in. I knew that from the first night I met him. But it doesn't stop me from wrapping my arm around him and getting a teensy tiny bit closer.

His entire body tenses for a split second before he relaxes into my embrace. He's slowly letting down his barriers.

"Look, I can't say that me and you are going to be forever. Or, that we're going to be anything more than what is happening while we're on this trip, but I do like you. You make me feel like my best self and that I can do anything I put my mind to."

"That's because you can," he responds.

"I wasn't done." I bop him on the nose, and he rears back a bit. "You're the one who told me to try things because you only live once, and life is too short. I am telling you that very same thing right now. Life is too short. We are obviously attracted to each other."

I can tell by the bulge in his sweat pants. He's not doing a very good job of hiding his lust.

"So, why not give this a shot?"

"I'm going to be real honest with you right now, Paula. You can always count on me, you know that. But if we do this, there's no way we can come out of this as friends. Not with any sort of attachment we have while we're here. Besides, your parents are right down the hall. What if they hear us?"

I lift my head and press a kiss to his cheek, then his chin, and lastly, his lips.

"I'm okay with that. Because I am doing the same thing. I am taking my shot and giving us a try."

I wait for a moment to see if he's going to say anything. When he doesn't, I continue. "If by the end of this weekend, and when we get back to Asheville, we realize it's not going to work, we'll deal with that then. But right now, you make me feel the best I've ever felt."

Finally, he wraps his arm around my waist and pulls me flush with his body.

"And your parents?"

I grin up at him. "I can be quiet."

Those last four words unleash whatever hold he had on himself. He buries his hand in my hair and smashes his lips into mine. His tongue caresses the seam of my mouth, asking permission.

That's the thing that I admire most about him. He will always wait until I give him the cues he needs to move forward.

Tongues swirling, I moan into his mouth. His answering groan sparks every atom in my body.

I slide my hand down his body and begin pulling at the waistband of his sweats.

He pulls away long enough to take off his shirt and throw it somewhere behind him. "Are you sure?"

I love that he's a gentleman, but right now, I need him to stop asking. Hell, I'm the one who instigated this, not the other way around. I nod. "Do you have protection?"

"Yeah." He chuckles nervously. "I wasn't expecting anything to happen, but I did come prepared."

It's good to know he wasn't completely against having sex when he came on this trip with me. I do respect him for having his boundaries even though I basically made him throw them out the window.

He slides off the bed and rushes to his bag to pull out a condom.

I grab the bottom of my shirt to take it off, but he whispers. "Don't."

"Why not?"

"Because I'm doing that."

I push my thighs together to try to dull the ache. But let's face it, nothing's going to cure this particular problem until he gets back in the bed.

He pushes his boxers down, kicking them off before ripping the condom packet open with his mouth and sliding it over his erection.

Thank God for moonlight is all I'm saying. The rest of the room is pitch black, and that somehow makes everything about this moment more special.

In two steps he's back at the bed, but instead of sliding in beside me, he guides me until I'm sitting up. He plays with the hem of my shirt before slowly lifting it over my head and tossing it over us.

His hand caresses my cheek, then down to my arm, before cupping my breast in his palm.

I've never been into foreplay, but he has me anticipating what his next move is going to be.

I fully expect his lips on mine, but when he leans over, he presses small kisses along my jaw line, before nibbling on my ear lobe. And good gravy, I did not know that was a turn on for me.

After a few seconds of teasing, his lips trail a line down my neck, my chest, before pulling my nipple into his mouth. His tongue swirls around my nipple once, twice before he gently nips it.

This isn't what I expected from mild mannered, polite Tristan. But I am happy I get to see this side of him.

Never in my life have I been with someone who is as intentional with my body as he is. It's almost as if he's worshipping me.

Cold air hits me and I realize his mouth is no longer there. He's now trailing kisses down my stomach before hooking his fingers in the waistband on my shorts and pulling them off along with my panties.

His mouth moves lower and lower until his tongue finds my clit. My hips buck up at the sudden sensation and I hold my breath to keep from letting out a whimper.

He moves lower still and his finger replaces his tongue. Nobody I've ever been with has made me feel as frantic or unhinged as I do right now.

I'm pretty sure this is what he meant by not being able to have sex without there being feelings attached.

Because those feelings, the need and want, are making this a thousand times better. Especially knowing that he's constantly putting me above anything else.

The motion of his fingers intensifies, and before long I'm squeezing my thighs to speed up my release.

A moan escapes my lips, and he uses his free hand to cover my mouth so I don't wake anybody up.

Now that my legs are no longer shaking, he moves from between my legs and hovers over me.

"You still good."

All I can do is nod my head. The rest of my body refuses to function.

He reaches between us, lining himself up with me, and takes his time as he pushes forward. Seconds ago, everything felt rushed and in the moment. But right now, every movement is slow, deliberate, and full of passion.

This is an entirely new experience for me, and I don't know how to handle it. My heart feels heavy and light at the same time. Something that has never happened. I'm not sure if it's a good thing or bad, but I can't deny I have more than friendly feelings toward this man.

Time ceases to exist and before I know it, I'm seeing stars. His mouth crashes into mine to swallow the sound. He follows soon after. Slowly he pulls away and lies next to me.

"I thought you said you can be quiet."

"Well, I wasn't expecting all of that." I wave toward his body.

"Me either." He laughs. "I'll be right back."

He puts on his pants and leaves the room. A few moments later he's back with a warm wash cloth. Even now he's making sure he takes care of me.

Now, that we're both cleaned up, we snuggle into each other. There's no more pretenses of pillow barriers. His arms are wrapped tight around me, and I fear I don't want to sleep without this feeling ever again.

tristan

PAULA. Has. Ruined. Me. That is my first thought as I wake up. I pat the space beside me, but she's not there. All I know is she didn't have any comments about being cold last night. Her wrapped in my arms as we fell asleep was a dream come true. Now, I need to figure out what time it is. Her brother didn't give us an exact time for when we're leaving.

I roll out of bed, and dig in my bag for a shirt. I can't leave the bed a mess and quickly make it before heading out of the room. That is one of the things the band gives me crap for. I always have to make my bed as soon as I get out of it.

Almost everyone is gathered at the dining room table. The only people missing are Phillip and Peter. I can't say I'm shocked after I had to tuck them in when we got home.

"Good morning, sunshine." Paula scoots over.

"Morning." This time it's my turn to kiss the top of

her head. My arms goes around her waist instinctively as soon as I sit down.

Both Parker and Piper giggle into their coffee cups. Dear God, I hope they didn't hear anything last night. They will never let us live it down. But it would squash any doubts they have about us being a couple.

I'm pretty sure that's what we are after her little talk last night. We should probably solidify that at some point today, for my own piece of mind.

Pierce is still sitting as far away from Paula as he can get, which isn't far at this table. We haven't had a meal at the same time, and I have no idea how everyone will fit when we do.

Abigail hands me a cup of coffee before heading back to the kitchen. "Thank you."

"Why do we have to leave so early?" Parker asks.

"Because the winery is just over an hour away, and they want us to come in early so we can talk about a potential partnership."

"I think it's dumb to partner with a competitor." Piper adds after taking a drink from her mug.

"We won't be carrying each other's wines, Piper." Pierce rolls his eyes. "We want to do an event together with maybe one other winery. If we all bring in our clientele, we can increase business all the way around."

"Is this one of those rising tides speeches?" Parker stands and heads to the kitchen. He begins helping Abigail with whatever she's making.

"It is unconventional," Paul says. "But new

marketing tactics won't kill us. Times are changing, and we need to as well."

Wow. That was…unexpected. I know most people are set in their ways when they've owned a business for a while. It's nice to see someone loosen the reins as they prepare to hand over their company.

Though, I have a feeling he won't completely retire. This family is too close knit and nosy for that to happen.

"Thanks for the vote of confidence, Dad." Pierce is beaming at his father's response. "We need everyone on board so we can hit the ground running."

I don't miss the pointed look he gives Paula. But she's not paying attention to anything he's saying.

She's whispering with her sister, and based the snickers, I have a feeling I know what it's about. This is humiliating. Next time Paula says she can be quiet, I'm going to call her a liar.

Abigail slides a plate of pancakes on the table at the same time Parker delivers bacon. She glances over at the plate and shakes her head. "There was more bacon than that."

Parker grins knowing damn well he's just been caught. "I don't know what you're talking about."

I've decided his charm is what keeps him out of trouble. I saw it in action when he was flirting with the bartender last night.

"How is everyone getting to the winery?" Paula asks now that she's done talking with Piper.

"We'll have to take two cars." Paul lifts a pancake off the plate and places it on the one in front of him. "We can figure out where everyone is going after breakfast. And after I drag your brothers out of bed."

Now it's his turn to shake his head at his children's shenanigans. He doesn't seem upset, though. His eldest son, however, glares at the hallway. He really needs to loosen up. I know they are doing some work on this trip, but it's also a vacation. People are allowed to go out and have fun.

"I'm riding with Paula." Both Piper and Parker announce at the same time.

"Well, that takes care of that." Paul laughs. "It looks like the last three will be close and personal in the truck's backseat."

I almost offer to take one of them, but it would be the same thing in Paula's car. The only different is, her backseat is smaller.

"Let's eat so we can get on the road." Pierce mumbles. "The other two will have to eat on the road."

Peter and Phillip are in for an earful when they get woken up. I'm glad I won't be in the vicinity. With any luck, we'll be on the road by then.

⁎

"I'm so glad we're done with that." Paula sighs as she slides into the passenger seat. I have to agree with her. The whole thing was boring. But, I'm not their demographic so my presence wasn't needed. The only reason I'm here is Paula.

"Speak for yourself." Piper moves into the backseat.

"I could have looked at their space all day. It's definitely giving me ideas for Starlit Fields."

"We should probably talk about the outside seating, too." Parker buckles his seatbelt.

I glance over at Paula as I turn on the car and put it in reverse. She looks like she wants to ask questions, but she keeps her mouth shut. It's natural she's curious, it's her family's business, but she made the rule about no winery talk with her younger siblings. It's a rule they all live by, and now that we're back on the road, the subject is changed.

I lay my hand on top of Paula's. She looks over at me. "Are you okay?" I mouth.

Her response is a nod. She'll say what she really thinks eventually, but she knows this car isn't a completely safe space, despite having Parker and Piper's support.

"What game are we playing tonight?" Parker asks.

I'm not sure who he's directing the question to. "What do you mean?"

"You know, family game night," Piper says as if that further explains it. "You know when most normal families play board, or card, games while laughing and smiling."

"Your family isn't normal?"

This time Paula busts out in laugher, leaning over until she can catch her breath. "I know you aren't serious with that question."

"Hey, I take offense." I can see Parker sit up straight in the rearview mirror. "I'm perfectly normal."

This time I join in the laughter. It feels good to be this relaxed in the car. Paula's rule is a smart one.

"You're probably the most not normal person in our family. Well, except maybe for Paula." Piper slaps her hands over mouth as soon as the words leave her mouth. "Shit. I'm sorry, Paula, I didn't mean it like that."

"I know, it's fine." Paula smiles at her sister, but I can see the pain behind her eyes. She doesn't like being singled out even if she doesn't want to be a part of the day to day. It's clear the distance she's put between herself and the winery also has ties into her relationship with her family. One of the many reasons I don't think someone should ever mix family and business. There are exceptions of course, but this isn't one of them. Paula ends up the ass end of all the jokes.

The only problem is nobody realizes she's not laughing.

Everyone at the table is staring at me. It doesn't seem to matter how many times they explain the rules, I can't keep up. At least they didn't have me take score. It would be a mess.

"What phase am I on?" I whisper to Paula.

She grabs the notebook from her mom, and studies the list of names. She smirks and hands it back.

"You're on phase two." She places a hand on my leg and squeezes. "If you need help all you have to do is ask."

"Do I have any shot at being anything other than dead last?"

She shakes her head. "Sorry. But I'm about to take some of these guys out."

"How do you pay attention to what's in your hand and what the others are playing? It's too much going on at once." Especially when you add in the noise. Everyone is talking over each other. Drinks are flowing. And I have no clue how I fit into game night.

We didn't do anything like this growing up. Family movie night was a tradition, but outside of that, nothing. As horrible as I am at playing a simple card game, I am enjoying myself.

"Hey," Piper raises her voice. "No whispering over there. We can't have you conspiring against the rest of us."

"Pfft. You're only saying that because you're just about tied with Tristan for last place." Phillip butts in. "Maybe try paying attention to what's going on around you instead of scrolling your phone."

"You. Are. Going. Down. Mister." She points at her brother and her cheeks flush a bright pink.

"Bring it on." He stands and motions to his sister. "Being the baby of the family won't save you tonight."

"Oh my gosh." Abigail shakes her head. "Phillip, sit down."

I wonder if this is what she meant when she said her family wasn't normal when it comes to game night. They are cutthroat when it comes to this game, and will distract each other to get the upper hand. Maybe it's like this for any games they play.

Was this what I was missing out on during my childhood? Honestly, seeing them all put their differences aside and have fun together while trying to destroy the other is heartwarming. Above all else they are family.

I know it's the same for my family, but it was never as loud as it is here. I have a few cousins my age, and we used to get together, except it was very chill. Everyone kind of did their own thing. We never played games or anything.

If there is anything I can compare this to, it's probably when I was in theatre. While it was fun, and loud, it wasn't a family unit.

Tonight makes me feel like I might want this in the future. The distant future, for sure, but a big family is appealing.

"Tristan, it's your turn." Parker nudges me.

"Oh, sorry." How did everyone go without me noticing? Oh, right, I was too busy being in my head instead of the moment.

I take a peek at the card with the phases listed and check my cards. Looks like I finally get to move on to the next phase.

LAST NIGHT WAS FUN. Pierce didn't bring up the winery once. I forgot what it's like to unwind with my family. We're actually a pretty lively bunch when we're not fighting amongst each other.

I'm feeling all the booze this morning, though. The will to leave my bed is long gone. I roll over, expecting to find an empty space beside me, but Tristan is there. Still sleeping. His face is relaxed, and he's softly snoring. Why is this man so adorable?

Never did I imagine I'd have these feelings for someone. I mean, I think I knew it *could* happen one day. But when we set out on this ruse, I never imagined actually falling for him. It seems too soon for him to completely turn my life upside down. Relationships are supposed to take time.

I remember Mom telling me Dad pursued her for months. She played hard to get so she would know he was serious about her. Apparently, Dad had a bit of a reputation before they got together and she was not messing around with her heart.

Tristan is nothing like that. He's been nothing but kind and considerate since I met him months ago. I've been the one consistently pushing him away, despite the sparks I felt hanging out with him that first night.

Ugh, this is why I don't do relationships. They make me question everything I thought I knew about myself.

"You look like you're contemplating your life choices." Tristan slides his arm around me, pulling me to him. He kisses my forehead and smiles down at me. "Good morning."

This may be my new favorite way to wake up. I'm in so much trouble. "Morning. I didn't wake you, did I?"

"No. I've been awake probably three times already, but I keep forcing myself back to sleep. Are you thinking about how bad of an idea it was to stay up until three drinking with your brothers? I know I am."

"No, I was barely buzzed." I snuggle into him. "I was thinking about us, and possibly freaking out a little bit."

"Why? We're still the same people, we're just officially dating now instead of it being a performance."

How pathetic will I sound if I tell him I've never actually dated anyone? Not even in high school. "Because I've never done this before. I wasn't lying when I said relationships weren't my thing."

"Well, they are now." He glances toward the window and the sunlight peeking through the blinds. "Do we have to be anywhere at a specific time today?"

"Not that I know of. Mom said something about

going to the botanical gardens at some point today. Why?"

"Come here." He lifts my chin and softly kisses me before tracing a line down my jaw.

"Absolutely not. We've already established I can't be quiet to save my life. And...I'm almost certain everyone is awake."

His chuckle vibrates through me. It's like a kitten's purr. "I wasn't going to suggest that. Well, I was...but you reminding me about the noise issue made me change my mind."

"Gee, thanks for the vote of confidence."

"It's not my fault." Another laugh. "Eh, maybe a little bit."

"You are definitely getting all the blame." I pull the covers over us more. "Why don't we go back to sleep for a while. It's so rare I get a chance to sleep in."

"That means you have to stop talking."

I pull my fingers across my lips as if I'm zipping them shut, and throw away the imaginary key.

This right here brings me the most comfort I've felt in a while. I feel safe and cared for. Tristan has my back no matter what. Even when I want to ignore the world for a while longer and drift off to dream land.

Something hits me in the head, and I sit up. "What the fuck?"

Piper is in the doorway with another pillow in her

hand. Peter is standing beside her with additional ammunition.

"Huh. The first pillow woke you up. I thought for sure I'd need at least three."

Peter laughs at our baby sister. He's not so bad as long as he's not up Pierce's ass, but right now I'm not amused with him.

"You never know, she might glare us to death and go back to sleep."

Tristan stirs beside me and slowly opens his eyes. "Why do I feel like we're under attack?"

"Because you are." Piper sing songs before chunking another pillow at us.

"Would you stop?" I growl. "We're awake."

"Good. It's after lunch. I know you weren't drunk when you went to bed last night. Why are you still in bed?"

I wave my arm around to show the room. "We're on vacation. That's what you're supposed to do."

"Except we're hungry." Peter whines. "Mom said we'd eat out for lunch before we go to the gardens. But you have to get up."

I swear some things never change. This brother of mine always thinks with his stomach. Tristan's stomach growls in response. Apparently, the mention of food reminds his body he hasn't eaten.

"Fine, we're getting up. Now go away."

"If I don't hear movement coming from this room in five minutes, I'm coming back with more pillows." Piper threatens. Tristan grins and my sister gags. "Don't be gross. Now get up and get ready. Mom won't let us leave until she knows y'all are at least in the process of getting dressed."

I throw the comforter off me and roll out of bed. "See, I'm up. You two can leave now."

"Fine, we're going." Piper holds her hands up in surrender. She mumbles something under her breath but I can't hear it.

As soon as the door closes, I let out a breath. "I swear sometimes I wish I was an only child. There wouldn't bet be all this pressure, and I wouldn't have siblings barging into my room unannounced."

"You don't mean that." Tristan gets out of bed and promptly makes it. I wonder why he didn't pick up the bedding off the floor the other day, if he makes the bed like this. Maybe he didn't want to wake me up. I don't know. But I already see an incompatibility issue because I'm not big on making it normally.

"I don't. I just wish they had some boundaries sometimes. They've always had a habit of just walking in. What if we'd been having sex?"

He stops what he's doing, walks over to me and wraps me in his arms. "I promise you, they'd be able to hear and wouldn't open the door."

I jab my finger into his side and he flinches. "Don't be a jerk. That's what I have siblings for."

"You're right." He holds me for a few more seconds before releasing me. "We should probably get ready before all of them attack."

"It'd be the last thing they ever do." I grin. "But,

yeah, we shouldn't keep them waiting. I'm gonna jump in the shower. If they come looking for me, tell them to chill."

"Like they'd listen to me," he mutters as I walk out of the bedroom.

My shower is quick. The last thing I want to do is make my family, and Tristan, wait longer than they need to. But I had to wash away last night's partying. It doesn't usually tire me out like that. But there was a ton of noise, and I need the time to decompress.

Parker is walking down the hall as soon as I open the bathroom door. "Please tell me you don't have to blow-dry your hair and do your makeup. I'm starving."

"Calm down." I shoo him away. "I just need to get dressed and put my hair in braids. I'm not trying to impress anyone.

"Not even Tristan?" He raises an eyebrow.

"I don't have to be all dolled up for him all the time. He likes me no matter how I look." I smile and move past him toward my room.

"Clearly he hasn't seen you after you've gotten drunk off your ass."

"Pfft. As if that happens often."

He taps his chin for a second, acting like he's deep in thought. "I seem to remember New Year's Eve a couple of years ago."

"We do not speak of that night. If you want me get ready really fast, you'll burn that night from your memories."

"You know what? You're right. It must have been

someone else." He continues down the hall. "Now hurry up."

I guess I have to keep my word now. Little brothers are so annoying.

When Mom said we were coming to the botanical gardens, I assumed everything would be dead, or near dying. They have a lot flowers inside this arboretum area where they cold won't get to them, and more of the native plants to the area outside.

It's really pretty here. I wonder why we haven't come before.

"Those are pretty," Tristan points to a flower. "They look like the ones used in the bouquet for Dale."

"Those are pincushions. Emily wanted to give his arrangement a little spark since it was for an engagement." It's pretty amazing I can recognize a lot of the flowers in here. My bosses would be proud of me. All their hard work training me is paying off.

"That's actually pretty cool. Do y'all customize like that for all holiday bouquets?" He's the first person outside of Parker and Piper who has asked me about my job. Even my parents haven't shown much interest. Which is kind of sad when I think about it.

"Usually only if the customer orders specific flowers to be added. But, if we know the occasion, we'll spruce it up. One of our customers gets their whole order customized for Valentine's Day."

"Why are they special?"

"Because it's Caroline's family, and she always goes above and beyond for them."

"I guess those are some of the perks of being related to amazing florists. I bet you make some beautiful arrangements."

"Not yet," I let out a breath. "They are teaching me, though. Each one I make gets better and better. Soon they'll be as show stopping as the others."

He slips his hand into mine. "I'll be your first order."

"You don't have to do that." I glance around to make sure nobody is around. "Besides who knows if we'll make it that long. You may get tired of me before then."

He pulls me to secluded area between flowers I don't recognize. "Don't put an expiration date on us when we've barely started. It's not fair to you or me."

"I don't think you realize how hard this is for me. To put my trust and heart on the line for someone."

He lifts a hand to my face, and I can't help but lean into him. "You don't have to worry about that with me. You *can* trust me. I only have your best interest at heart. There's nothing I would intentionally do to hurt you."

"You shouldn't make promises you can't keep."

"Then I guess, I'll have to prove it to you." He leans forward and presses a kiss to my forehead. That small action may be my new favorite thing in the world. It's sweet and tender. He treats me like I'm precious. Maybe he will make good on everything he says.

tristan

I HEAR a click and turn toward the area Paula and I were standing in before I pulled her aside. Piper is standing with her phone lifted in her hand. It's pointed directly at us.

Paula turns to see what caught my attention. "What the hell?"

Her sister's eyes are wide, and she knows she fucked up. "I'm sorry, I wasn't trying to intrude."

"Well, you sure seem like you're fine with butting in on private moments." Paula pulls away from me. Our little bubble of solitude has burst and her guard has gone up once again.

"I didn't mean to interrupt you. I turned the corner and y'all looked adorable. I only wanted to capture the moment for you." She lowers her hand and slides her phone into her pocket. "I really am sorry."

Those are her last words before she runs off. I'm not

upset. Her intentions were good, but even I know the invasion of privacy isn't something Paula enjoys.

With her sister gone, she buries her face in her hands. "What is with her always trying to capture everything on her phone? I don't understand it. Sometimes you need to live in the moment."

I bend down until I can see her face. Well, her hands and slowly move them away. "She was trying to capture memories. I'm sure she didn't mean anything by it."

"That's not the point."

"I know." I give her hands a soft squeeze. "Dale felt the same way when he'd look into the crowd and see phones instead of faces. It really bugged him. But I told him the same thing. His fans may only be able to see the band once in their lifetime. Those videos and photos are proof of their experience. Something they'll look back on and cherish. She probably thought the same thing."

"Why do you always have to be so rational?"

"With Dale, that's what I'm paid for." I let go of her hand and wrap my arm around her waist. "For you, it's so you can see the good parts of your family. They aren't always coming at you for something to do with the business. They genuinely like having you around."

I lead us out of the small alcove. "And because I know the importance of keeping record of memories. All I have left of my grandparents are photos. Even though it's sad sometimes, I love looking at them. You can see the love emanating from them, even in the candid shots."

This time she stops our movement, and wraps both arms around me. "I'm sorry. I didn't know."

"It's okay." I assure her. "It never came up."

"No, but I feel like a shitty person now." She buries her face in my shirt. It's another tell I'm picking up from her when she feels like she can't control a situation. "You know all this stuff about me, and I barely no anything about your family outside of your parents and brother. Even that is bare minimum."

"It's fine." I rub small circles on her back. "We have time to learn more about each other. Besides, I don't know much about your family, either." When we were still a fake couple, we kept everything surface level. It was my insistence to keep my feelings in check. Now, we have the opportunity to really get to know each other.

"When we get back to Asheville, we're going on a proper date without my meddling family around."

"That's a promise." I laugh. "Let's find the rest of the group."

Hopefully, she can clear the air with her sister. She's so used to being treated like the outcast because she doesn't want the same things that her first instinct is to go into defense mode. Hopefully, that can change before we leave. We only have one more full day, and I want them all to be on the same page.

Not for them, but for Paula. She needs to know her family has her back even if she's not working for Starlit Fields.

"You want to help with the grill?" Peter asks as I come into the kitchen.

"Sure." Luckily, I know what I'm doing when it comes to grilling. It's one of the things my dad had me help him with when I was living at home.

Mom always did theatre and music things with me. With Dad, we grilled and watched football. He'd come to my shows, but he didn't have the same passion for it my mom did. Well, still does. She always asks if I want to see a play if the stars align while I'm in town.

"You may want to get a jacket before we head out there. We have the outdoor heater, but it's still chilly."

"I'll be right back."

I rush down the hallway and to our room. That has a nice ring to it. Too bad it's only ours one more night. At least then we can have some privacy.

Paula is sitting on the bed with her phone in her hands.

"What are you looking at?"

She looks up, teary-eyed, and wipes her face. "It's the picture my sister took."

"Wow. It's so bad it's making you cry?" I sit down next to her. "It's because of me, right?"

"No, weirdo." She smacks my chest. "It's not because of you. It's a really great picture."

I don't make any movements to let her have her moment. It must be a really good picture if she's rendered speechless.

"Can I see it? Or, are you keeping it a secret from me."

She laughs before leaning on my shoulder. "I'm not keeping it to myself. Just savoring the moment."

"Did you and Piper talk?" Honestly, the picture doesn't mean as much to me as her relationship with her sister. She's one of the few siblings Paula is close to. I know arguments happen in families, but I think if everyone here talked more, there wouldn't be so many hard feelings toward each other.

"Yeah." She nods. "It was exactly like you said. She thought it was something we would cherish. I apologized so much for flying off the handle. She's the one I trust most in this family and I treated her like crap."

"As long as things are good between you now, then I'd say it was a good talk."

"Yeah, we're cool. Lucky for me, she knows I only need time. She was more embarrassed because you're the one who caught her taking the picture."

"I'm used to it." I wave the comment away. "I'm sure some of Crooked Halo's fans have some pretty horrible pictures of me."

"But this isn't horrible." She grabs her phone and lifts it to my face. "It's perfect."

She's not wrong. The sun is illuminating us through the windows and she caught the exact moment I kissed Paula's forehead. If you didn't know better, you'd think it was a posed picture. This photo is something I'll treasure for a long time.

Despite the meltdown she was having, she looks comfortable and completely at ease in my embrace. People say a picture is worth a thousand words, but this one leaves me without them. All I see is adoration and the inkling of something more. Something I don't want to put a name to because I know Paula will think it's too early for those kind of declarations. But when you know, you know. And I know without a doubt I'm falling head over heels for her.

"Can you send that to me?"

"Yeah." She presses a few buttons and my phone dings in my pocket. "Why were you rushing in here?"

"Oh, I was getting a jacket. Peter's probably waiting on me."

"For what?"

"Grilling dinner."

She bursts out laughing and doubles over. "That's because he burns everything. He needs someone to blame it on, or take over the job."

"Oh, I didn't realize that."

"It's not something he advertises." She regains control of herself. "Do you know how to grill?"

"As a matter of fact. I do."

"Thank God. The food will be edible." She pushes me off the bed. "You better go so he doesn't ruin it for everyone."

I give her a quick kiss before grabbing my jacket and hightailing it out of the room. Is he really that bad of a cook? Surely not.

Parker is in the dining area opening up a bottle of beer, but I don't see his brother anywhere.

"Where's Peter?"

"He went outside with the steaks. Please save them."

Geez, he doesn't have any fans of his cooking. Maybe it's a good thing I decided to help him out.

"Thanks." I slip my jacket on and head outside.

Sure enough, Peter is standing in front of the grill, except the steaks are nowhere in sight.

"I went ahead and got them started. You were taking a bit."

The flames are as high as the lid of the grill. He really doesn't know what he's doing. "The flame is too high."

"What?"

"The flame is too high. The steaks will burn before the middle gets to the right temperature." Thanks Pops for that little tidbit of information when I was a teen.

"No problem. And sorry about taking so long. I was talking with Paula." More like admiring the photo from earlier. I pull my phone out of my pocket to save it. I also make it my wallpaper while I have it pulled up.

"She's different," Peter says. His focus is on the grill.

"Who?" I know who he's talking about, but I want him to come out and say it. He's one of the brothers she's not very close to, and I want to get a handle on what he thinks and feels.

"Paula. Not in a bad way, or anything like that. But she's usually way moodier and meaner on game nights. She actually seems to be enjoying her time with us."

"That's good, right?" I don't see where he's going with this.

"Yeah, I think a lot of it has to do with you." He shakes his head. "She's never brought a guy around. Hell, half the time she doesn't show up unless she's forced to. Then she's in a bad mood the entire time."

This is one of those moments where it's hard to keep my mouth shut. I want to tell them it's because they put too much pressure on her. That they don't value what makes her unique. But I can't, not yet. It's not my place. But the day is coming when I'll let my thoughts be known.

"I'm sure she has her reasons."

"Yeah, I can't really blame her." He glances over at me before moving toward the heater. "Pierce is kind of a dick at times. But that's how big brothers are supposed to be to the younger kids."

I don't know where he got that warped sense of thinking. My brother has never treated me the way I've seen Pierce treat Paula.

"It wouldn't be so bad if he didn't single her out." I've noticed he's hard on the rest of them, but her especially.

"Yeah, I don't know why he's like that with her. I do my best to do what he asks. If I do it, then he can't complain about it."

How sad is it that they have this view of their brother? I don't think it's something Pierce learned from his own father. Paul has been nothing but kind and outgoing. He hasn't even brought up the winery with Paula since we've been here. I feel like Pierce is putting the pressure on her saying it's coming from their parents. That will end up biting him in the ass one day.

"I get it. My brother was already in college by the

time I was a pre-teen. So, we didn't really grow up in the same house."

He laughs. "What's that like? I can't imagine not having my brothers and sisters pestering me all the time."

"Lonely, mostly." I grab the spatula and flip the steaks. "I had friends, but when it was time for them to go home, I didn't have anyone."

"I don't envy you."

"You shouldn't."

We watch the steaks a little longer. They should be just about done. The wind picks up and the salt on the breeze is heavy. As much as I'm enjoying the beach, I don't think I could live here full time.

"Do you want a beer?"

"Sure."

He reaches into a small cooler and pulls out a bottle before handing to me. Maybe Paula's family is a tad out of touch with who she is, but they do pay attention. I think she'd like to know that. But, it should come from them. Not me. It'll make more of an impact on her.

"HOW DO you feel about a walk on the beach?" Tristan asks as we're watching a movie in the living room. Half of my siblings are on one sofa and, and the others are out. I don't know if they are with Mom and Dad, but there are only five of us here.

"Isn't it still cold outside?" Honestly, I want to hang out on the sofa all day. This weekend has been so busy. We've done something each day, and being lazy sounds like the perfect way to end this trip. Though I am wondering where my parents ran off to.

"I don't mean right now." He pulls me closer to him. This is the moment I don't want to break. The comfort of being in his arms is more than I ever imagined this could feel like. "It's supposed to get warmer. I was thinking in a couple of hours."

"Okay. It'll give us time to finish this movie." I have no clue what's going on in the movie. It's weird and doesn't make any sense. We should never let Phillip pick the movie. You'd think we'd learn that by now. I'm sure he loves the movies he decides on, but they aren't exactly what everyone else likes. Sci-fi movies just aren't my thing.

"This battle scene is epic," Phillip whispers. His eyes are wide and laser focused on the TV.

Piper busts out laughing. "This entire movie is corny as hell. The graphics aren't even that great."

"Beauty is in the eye of the beholder," Parker argues. "This is his happy place, don't ruin it."

"I guess," she mutters as she crosses her arms over her chest. I'm with her. I don't understand what's so fantastic about this movie. But, he got to the TV first.

One of these days my parents will pick a rental that has TV's in the bedrooms. I get why they don't because we'd all ditch each other to do our own thing. But it'd be nice to be able to zone out to our favorite shows when being around everyone gets to be too much. The forced bonding time can bit a bit too much.

"Sometimes it's about the storytelling." Phillip pleads his case. "I've seen some of the stuff you watch, and it doesn't appeal to me, but it has you hooked. It's not a bad thing to expand your horizons."

"Can we all just watch the movie?" I groan. If I don't put an end to this conversation, it'll turn into a debate and ruin the lazy mood.

"Thank you, Paula," Phillip says. I didn't do it so he could enjoy it, but so this doesn't turn into a whole thing. It's not something I feel like dealing with this morning, and I won't allow bickering to overtake the morning.

"Hey," Tristan whispers in my ear. "The movie is over."

"Huh?" I open my eyes and see him leaning over me. I guess I feel asleep. The last thing I remember is watching a fight on screen, apparently the movie is full of those. It was like I blinked and it was over.

"The movie is over, and you'll be happy to know there wasn't any more fighting."

"That's good." I sit up and rub my eyes. "We can go on that walk now. I need to move my body."

"I'll grab our jackets in case we need them." He moves out from beside me and heads toward the room.

My body feels stiff and I stand, stretching my arms over my head. This is why I stopped falling asleep on the sofa. My body always feels like it's been in a ten round fight. I refuse to believe it's because I'm getting older. Maybe this is the argument I'll give Mom for the next vacation spot to have a TV in the room.

Tristan comes back into the room, with jackets in hand. "Are you ready to head out?"

"Yep." I move toward him and he helps me into the jacket. It doesn't matter if it's warmed up outside, I'm always cold so I'll need it.

"That was an impressive move earlier to keep them from fighting," he opens the door for us to go out. The door clicks shut behind us. "I need to use those tactics to keep the band in line."

"You pick up a thing or two when you're an older sibling. I try to be nicer, but they were going to ruin the vibe so I had to be a little more authoritative. They don't like when I put on the mean big sister hat."

"Sometimes you have to do things people don't like."

We move toward the beach and turn left. It's opposite from the direction I took the other day. I know his words are meant to remind me I need to tell my family I don't want to take part in the business, but I don't want to get into that right now.

We walk in silence for a bit. There are more people on the beach today. Nobody is in the water, of course, but couples walk hand in hand and kids are building sand castles, doing their best not to get wet. It feels like the area is coming to life after the cold snap the past few days.

Tristan breaks the silence. "I know you don't like talking about the future, but when we get back to Asheville, we're still going to be a couple, right?"

The doubt in his voice hits me in the heart. "Yes. I told you, I'm stepping out of my comfort zone. We can see how we are together without my family surrounding us. I want to know how we can be when it's just us."

He lets out a breath. "Good. We'll have to figure out how things will work when Crooked Halo goes on tour again, but that's not for a long time. They are happy to take time off from touring, and hanging out in the new house they bought."

"Are you going to live with them?" It'll be hard to have alone time in a house full of people.

"I may have to for a little bit, but I'm hoping that's not the case. I love those guys, but I can't live with them long term after seeing them on the road day in and day out."

"Do you know what kind of place you're looking for? I can help you look." If anything, I'm sure my friends and coworkers know of some places. They are more connected to what's going on in town than I am.

"Probably an apartment for now." He runs a hand through is hair. "I would look for a house, but I don't want to rush into that. It's a big investment, and I want to make sure it's something I'll love."

"Makes sense." I nod in agreement. "The complex Angie lived in is nice."

"Cool. I'll get the information from her."

That seems to conclude our talk of the future for now. It's not something we need to worry about. We said we were going to take things one day at a time. Looking too far forward is terrifying. As much as I want to think this could be the real thing and last forever. I still have to protect my heart...even though it's losing the battle and falling for him each passing moment.

He takes his jacket off and lays it on the ground before taking a seat. He pulls me down in front of him and cradles my body with his. The sound of the waves rolling over each other, and families playing is just what I need to calm any doubts and fears I have it. It's uncanny how well he reads me, and know what I need before I do.

"There you are." Mom's voice pulls me out of the moment. I'm not sure how long we've been out here. I didn't think to grab my phone. I didn't want to be interrupted by anyone, but it seems they sought us out anyway.

Shielding my eyes from the sun, I glance up. It's not only my mom, but the entire freaking family.

"What did you do? Form a search party?"

"Sort of?" Piper shrugs her shoulders. "You didn't answer your phone, and figured out here was the best bet of finding you. Plus, I knew y'all were going to be out here somewhere. It was a matter of picking a direction."

My sister knows me too well. "Well, you found us. What's up?"

This time Peter comes to the front with a football in his hand. He tosses it up and catches it. "How about a friendly game of football?"

"You brought a football with you?" It shouldn't be shocking. Outside of working, the only thing he loves more is sports.

"No." He shakes his head. "I bought it when we were out earlier."

"You realize none of us are as young as we used to be, right? We can't be tackling each other to the ground. We might break something."

He extends his hand to help me up. "You're only as old as you feel. But we'll keep it flag so we don't accidentally take each other out."

I let him pull me up, and I can feel Tristan stand behind me. "We don't have any—"

He cuts me off, letting go of my hand, he pulls something out of his pocket. They are thin strips of fabric with velcro on the ends. "You were saying?"

"Smart ass," I mumble. All it does is make him laugh. He knows I hate when he's thought of everything. Apparently, all my siblings know me better than I thought they did, even the ones I'm not as close to. "How are we going to divide up in teams?"

Growing up when we did things like this, we always had the same dynamic. Me, Piper and Parker against Pierce, Peter and Phillip. It used to irritate Phillip when he'd be stuck on Pierce's team.

"Since I'm the odd one out, I'm picking the teams." Mom says. "No offense, but I don't trust any of you to not accidentally knock me down."

She's a smart woman. It wouldn't be intentional, but we have a habit of getting rowdy when we're trying to win. It's the competitive nature all of us share. I'm almost certain it's a trait we got from Dad.

"Tristan, Piper, Peter and Paul. The four of you are on a team."

"Wait," I blurt out. "Dad's playing?"

"How could I miss out on this?" He laughs at me. "Y'all are going down."

"Oh my God, Dad. Don't ever say that again." Parker groans. "You sound like you're trying to be young and cool."

"I am young and cool. You can't deny it."

Well, at least we know where Parker gets being full of himself from.

"Y'all take a few minutes to get ready." She points at Tristan's jacket and asks, "Is it okay if I sit here?"

Tristan rushes over to her. "Yes, ma'am. Do you want me to shake some of the sand off?"

"It's fine. It's not like there won't be more." She sits down and crosses her legs in front of her. I've never seen her sit like that in my adult years. It's weird and she looks childlike.

As stressful as this trip has been on me mentally, I'm glad we're all coming together like this, even if I am on a team with Pierce. This is where it'll get interesting.

I motion for my brothers to gather around. "Okay, who are we targeting?"

"My money is on Piper. You know she sucks at sports," Parker says.

"Oh, I was going to say Dad. I've never once in my life seen him play anything."

"Don't discount him too easily," Pierce replies. "He does a lot of the heavy lifting at the winery."

I didn't know that. "Why? Shouldn't one of y'all be doing it?"

"Because he's as stubborn as a damn mule." Parker states. "We tell him we'll get it and he sends off to do something else so he can handle it. It's no wonder all of us are the way we are."

He's not wrong on that aspect. I thought for a second Pierce was going to add some bullshit about me coming back to work there, but he didn't. He let it go for now.

"Okay, so Dad's out. I'm not sure how Tristan is with sports. I know he was in theatre in high school. He also lifts and moves around the equipment for Crooked Halo. So, he might have braun, but I don't know if he has speed."

Pierce lifts his head to see what the other team is doing and then comes back to us. "Okay, we're going to need some man-on-man defense. Parker, you need to stick with Piper. She doesn't think you'll take her flag since you're the next youngest."

"She should know better." Parker grins and claps his hands together. He's about to make her life hell.

"Phillip, you've got Dad. I've got Peter in case he forgets we're playing flag football. Paula, you're on your boyfriend." He puts his hand in the middle and waits for all of us to join him. "Remember, we go for the win. No emotions"

"Got it." We lift our hands in the air and take our positions in front of the rest of our family.

Tristan thought we got excited when we play cards. He has no head what's about to happen. He should be lucky he got me. I know Pierce said no emotions, but I can't throw him into this without some sort of warm up.

Mom cups her hands over her mouth. "Are y'all ready?" After we all nod, she grins. "Let the game begin."

We don't bother flipping a coin to see who gets the ball first because we know Peter isn't going to let go of it until he snaps it to one of his players. He bends over and calls out some ridiculous sounding play and hikes it to Dad.

Piper runs toward the outside with Parker on her heels. Pierce is trying to keep Peter from getting the ball again. Apparently, they picked the same line up as we did because Tristan is waiting to see where the ball goes. Dad over throws it to him and it's my time to shine.

I rush to get it, but Tristan is right there in front of me, reaching for the ball. I lose my footing and fall backward. He continues running with the ball. I guess he got the no emotions memo.

tristan

BY THE TIME we get back to the beach house, we are sweaty and sandy. Even though it was flag football, a couple of us forgot. Mostly Peter. I can't count how many times he tackled Pierce and Parker. I think it was brotherly fun, but I can never tell. A completely different side comes out when this family plays anything. It's not just card games where they try to take each other out.

"Everyone needs to get cleaned up while I get dinner started." Abigail announces before we walk inside.

"I'm not using this outside shower to get the sand off," Piper says as she opens the door.

"Then you're sweeping it all up afterward. You know sand tracks everywhere no matter what you do."

"I'm okay with that. It's too cold out here to be getting soaking wet." She walks inside, leaving the door open.

I move toward the outside shower, and Paula places a

hand on my arm. "We'll help her clean up. She's right about the cold."

The chill of the evening hits the sweat on my skin and goosebumps form along my arm. "Okay, I can live with that."

There are only two showers so it takes a while. Hopefully there's enough hot water for all of us. Both Piper and Paula have long hair, and I know it will take a while for them to get it all out.

Everyone is in their respective areas. Some are waiting on a shower and some are cleaning up. I'm part of the latter. Paula tried to get me to join in the shower with her, but it felt inappropriate with her family here.

I pull the laundry bag I brought with me out of my duffel. Gathering up my dirty clothes is kind of a pain. Normally I would do this as I'm changing, but this weekend has been a whirlwind...both emotionally and physically. But I know the plan is to leave early in the morning, and I want to make sure all of my stuff is ready to go. The only thing I have going for me with this task is my stuff is in one central location.

Paula will have a more difficult time. She has stuff scattered around the room. A part of me wonders if her house is this chaotic, or if it's only specific areas that aren't seen by everyone. I've only seen her living room and kitchen. I made sure everything else was off limits because I didn't want to go down that road before I knew her better. One-night stands are something I just don't do. I've never judged anyone who prefers them. Hell, I didn't say anything untoward to Paula that first night. I told her what I was okay with and asked if she was in or not. Luckily for me, she was in.

The door opens and the woman in question strides inside wearing nothing but a towel. Too bad I'm disgusting right now because I'd suggest some things.

"Are you trying to leave early?" She asks while taking the towel out of her hair and dropping it to the floor.

"Nope. I'm getting things ready for in the morning." I place the laundry bag next to my duffel. "I don't want to forget anything, or be rushed."

She looks around the room at her things strewn about. "That's a good idea, I should probably do the same."

"Possibly." I move toward her and begin sliding my arms around her before she slaps my hands away.

"I just finished getting all the sand off me. I'm not letting you put it all back." She crosses her arms over her chest, defiant. Her being this way with me gives me hope she'll have the same confidence when confronting her family. "Also, I didn't tell anyone I was out of the shower, and they didn't see me. If you want to jump in while there's still hot water, now's your chance."

"Thanks." I give her a quick kiss before grabbing my clothes off the bed. "I think this proves you like me more than you like your family."

"Maybe a little." She uncrosses her arms and pinches her fingers together to show just how much she likes me.

"Keep lying to yourself." I slip out of the room before she has a chance to make a smartass comeback.

The water doesn't take long to get warm when I turn

it on. I drop my clothes on the counter before undressing and getting in the shower. My main focus is my hair. There's no telling how much sand is trapped in it, and I want to get that clean first. It doesn't take long since I have way less hair than the women in this family. I also don't want to be the jerk that uses all the hot water.

Within ten minutes I'm out of the shower and drying off. Maybe the brothers will be happy I saved them some. It'll definitely increase their good will toward me. Today was a milestone in my opinion. They acted as if I was a part of the family, and not an outsider. They've tried to include me each day I've been here, but today I felt welcomed. Even Pierce was nice to me. I thought he was still upset about me going off on him the other day. Hopefully he knows my heart is in the right place but now, I won't do anything to upset Paula.

When I get back to the room, Paula is shoving things into her bag. "Do you need some help?"

She turns around and one of her braids hits her in the face. She slaps it away, and shakes her head. "I don't think so. I think I got most of my stuff."

I grab discarded shirt from the dresser. "Are you sure?"

"Damn it." She grabs it from my hand and puts it in her bag. "Okay, so maybe I do need help."

"Make sure you leave your pajamas and clothes for tomorrow out. Otherwise, you'll have to dig them out later."

"How are you so good at all this stuff? Any time I go on a trip I swear I leave half my stuff."

I'm walking around the room, picking up whatever I find. "Traveling with a band can be chaotic at best. When we're constantly on the move, I have to do what I can to keep organized. I figured that out after I lost a few things when I started working for them. Some of them were pricey items and it didn't take long to learn my lesson."

"It's smart," she agrees. "I wish I was more like that sometimes. This is pretty much what my room looks like at home. Half the time I can't find anything. I need to get things organized."

So, I was right. She keeps the community spaces clean and lets herself go in the other areas. "You shouldn't change how you do things because you're impressed by the way I do them. But if you really want me to help you, I will."

"Thanks." She smiles at me. "If I can get a process started, I can stick to it."

"Most people operate that way. When things are messy, they get overwhelmed and don't know where to start."

"Well, you're going to help me get back on track."

There are footsteps coming down the hall then they stop right outside our door. "Dinner's ready. Y'all come eat."

Abigails voice is loud enough to be heard by everyone. Unless they are in the shower. Hopefully everyone is done with those.

"Was your mom a cheerleader, or someone who had to get people's attention?"

"She wasn't, but she did have to wrangle all of us at once. She's learned to be loud when she needs to be."

"Makes sense." I set the few things I've picked up on the bed. "Let's go eat."

We head to the dining area and I'm shocked to find everyone already there. Not much time has passed since Abigail told us to get in here. I swear this family can be stealthy when they want to be.

The table is already set. We take our seats where we've been sitting while here. There is food everywhere covering every inch of space.

"Mom, why is there so much of everything?" Paula asks as she takes a drink of the tea sitting in front of her spot.

"These boys didn't eat as much as they usually do, and we need to get rid of some of this food."

"Oh." Paula looks at each dish on the table. "It's like the holidays but not. I'll gladly take some leftovers home if there are any."

"I guess it's a good thing I brought some bowls."

We all load up our plates and dig into the food. For once nobody is talking over another person. It was probably playing football that made everyone so hungry. Working concerts is hard work, but I haven't run around like that in a long time. I should definitely add physical activity back into my routine. I feel good now even if I'll probably be hurting tomorrow.

Once everyone is done eating, we help clear away the dishes and clean the kitchen. All hands are on deck, and it doesn't take long for the kitchen to be back in pristine condition. Paul grabs a couple bottles of wine and brings them into the living room where we've moved.

"I hope everyone has had fun this weekend," he smiles as he opens it and pours it in the glasses Abigail brought from the kitchen.

"It's been a blast," Piper adds as she takes the glass of wine he offers her. "It's been a while since we were all under one roof."

Everyone glances toward Paula knowing she's the missing link when it comes to get togethers. I know she can feel their eyes on her. She doesn't turn away from the scrutiny, though.

"As you can tell from earlier today, I'm not getting any younger. I will be retiring soon, and I want to say how happy I am I'm leaving our family legacy in capable hands."

"Are you retiring tomorrow or something?" Parker asks, confused.

"No," Paul laughs. "I'm not retiring tomorrow. It will still be a while. I need to get documents for the lawyer and all that stuff. I just want y'all to know you're going to do a great job with Starlit Fields."

Pierce stands up next to his dad. Did they rehearse this? Maybe that's what they were doing when they were gone earlier today.

"We'll do you proud, Dad." He claps his dad on the back. "We'll need all hands-on deck when the time comes. I have areas I want each person involved in."

His siblings are looking at him like he's lost his marbles because they are already immersed in the business. This is all for show for one person and I hate that he's singling her out like this.

"Paula, I hope you'll consider being a part of our legacy. It means a lot to all of us to have you on board. We're family and it should be family who continues this business."

The rest of her siblings shift uncomfortably. Even Paul takes a step back and stares at his feet. Is he intimidated by his own son? Abigail twists her hands in her lap and shakes her head.

Paula glances at me. For support, or to speak up for her, I don't know. But I can't fight this battle for her. She needs to do it on her own.

"Pierce, I appreciate that you want me to help, but I have a job. I like what I do."

"But that isn't where you belong," he argues and takes a step forward. "This is what we've always known we were supposed to do."

Paula takes a moment to look at each of her siblings, then her parents, studying their expressions. All of them seem to be embarrassed but also hopeful. She doesn't acknowledge me, though.

She turns her focus to her big brother. "I'll think about it. Will that satisfy you for now?"

He nods. "We have time. I only wanted to see where you stand."

"Thanks."

She doesn't argue with him, or tell him how she really feels about working in the winery. She gives him an answer to put it off. All this tells me is she will likely end up doing something she isn't passionate about to appease her family.

After everything she's told me, she still can't stand up to them. It looks like they were getting into a much better place. Like maybe Pierce wasn't going to put pressure on her to do this. I know I said I wasn't going to fight her battles for her, but damn it. I can't let her do this. But I'm not an asshole, unlike her brother. I'll wait until we're alone to see what the hell she's thinking. Until we go to bed, the only thing I can do is grin and bear it.

CHAPTER NINETEEN

LEAVE it to my brother to single me out in front of everyone. I don't know why I expected any less. This was exactly the kind of thing he would do. He knows I won't say no in front of everyone. I felt Tristan's body stiffen the moment I said I'd think about it.

A small part of me thought he'd step in. That he'd tell my brother where to shove it, but he didn't. It's not his fault. He told me he wouldn't. He said he'd be by my side for support, but I would have to take the last steps on my own.

"I'm gonna hit the hay," Dad says and stands. "We have to be out of here early in the morning and I don't want to wake up late."

The rest of us follow suit. Mom grabs the glasses off the coffee table and takes them to the kitchen. Piper jumps up to help her. Maybe she feels the tension hanging in the air since Pierce's little speech, despite all of us doing our best to ignore it.

Tristan and I head to our room. As much as I want to delay the inevitable, I know there's about to be a showdown. I only hope we can come through it without destroying the both of us.

I walk into the room and begin putting away the things gathered earlier. The drive home is going to be awkward no matter what happens tonight, and I want to get out of here as soon as possible. If it wasn't so late, I'd suggest we leave tonight. Forget that little comment ever happened.

The door clicks shut behind me. It takes him all of two seconds to open his mouth. "What the hell was that?"

"Do we really have to do this right now?"

"When else do we suggest we discuss it?" He's frustrated, and I don't blame him. I would be if the roles were reversed.

"I would be good if we never brought it up again. It's not like I'm going to go through with it." I keep packing as if there isn't a five hundred pound weight on me.

"That's too bad, Paula." I feel his hands on my shoulders, but he doesn't force me to turn around. He's waiting for me to take the step. Even when he's upset with me, he doesn't force anything on me.

"Look, I know that didn't go down how either of us wanted, but he put me on the spot. What was I supposed to do?"

As much as I want to turn around, let him wrap his arms around me, and comfort me, I won't. Mostly because I can't stand to see the disappointment, I know is written all over his face. I'm the one who put it there, and I don't have the stomach to face the fact I disappointed yet another person.

"You were supposed to tell them you don't want to be a part of the company."

"It's not that easy when your entire family is in the room." As much as he's trying to help, this isn't something he'll ever understand. He doesn't have a massive family. He also doesn't have a family that's owned a company for multiple generations. The ability to stand up to all of them at once is terrifying.

"I get th—"

"No, you don't." How could he? "When you've been in the same position as me, then you can have commentary on how I handle it."

He says nothing and I know I've punched him in the gut. Now, I turn around. I need to see him.

"Damn it, Paula. I'm not trying to be like your brother. But that was part of the deal. You would finally stand up for yourself."

So, he was waiting until he had my full attention to act like an ass.

"That deal was while we were a *fake* couple." The agreement should have been off the table once we became official. "I still plan on telling them, just not right now. I couldn't let what was actually a decent weekend end on a bad note."

"Instead, you'll give them false hope that you'll put aside your passions to fulfill theirs. Tell me how that makes any kind of sense. There are going to be hurt feelings either way. At least here, you have them all in one spot so you can open up conversation. And I'm here to give you the support you need for it."

"How will that be different once we're home?" I don't see the issue. Except maybe the fact I'm going back on my word twice. First to him, and then to my family once I come clean about my intentions.

Leave it to me to screw this up so badly because I don't like confrontation. Well, unless it's with Tristan, because he is the only person I trust to be on my side at the other end of the disagreement.

He shakes his head. "It wouldn't be. I'd still have your back. But you won't be able to move past everything until you talk it out with them. Here, you can say your piece at one time. When we're back home…who knows when you'll get everyone together in one place?"

He takes a step toward me, and I take a step back. He's not wrong, and it's infuriating. "Can we talk about this tomorrow? It's a long drive, and I'm ready for bed."

I don't give him a chance to respond. I put the stuff in my hands in my suitcase and grab my jammies. The last hour has been mentally exhausting, and I don't have it in me to keep going with this argument.

"Yeah, fine." The defeat in his voice breaks my heart. He's very much the type of person who wants to finish things. He doesn't like things unresolved and out in the open. But I can't give him that tonight.

With my clothes in hand, I walk around him to the

door before pausing. I want to tell him I'm still all in with him. That the bullshit with my family is my burden to carry, and I want him there to support me at every stage. But, I don't.

I turn the knob, make sure nobody is standing outside my door, and walk out of the room. I wouldn't put it past my younger siblings to stand on the other side to see what is going on. They knew something was amiss when we all went to bed, since some of them know how I feel.

I take my time changing into my pajamas, anything to prolong going back into the room too quickly. Could I have changed in the room? Yes. Except I need some space right now and time to be alone with my thoughts. He wasn't wrong with anything he said.

If I was a stronger person, I would have told my brother where to shove it and I wouldn't be fighting with the person who now holds my heart. As much as I want to be this larger-than-life version of myself, it will take time. For now, I'm still the little sister getting pushed around by her big brother.

Deep breath in and out. It's just one more night and then I won't see everyone for a bit. I can think of how I'll tell Pierce I'm not stepping up to work in the company. But right now, I need to make peace with the way I handled everything.

When I get back to the room, I don't see Tristan in bed. Did he go outside for fresh air while I was in the bathroom? I move to my suitcase to add the clothes I changed out of to the pile.

That's when I see the corner of the blanket on the floor. My steps are soft and slow as I move to the other side of the bed. Tristan has made his bed on the floor once again. I guess I upset him more than I thought.

Tiptoeing around to the other side of the bed, I slide under the comforter. It feels lonely without him snuggled up next to me. Who knew I could become comfortable sleeping beside someone in such a short amount of time?

I take a few moments to place some pillows on the side he occupied, trying to feel that peace I had. It doesn't work. Cold pillows are nothing compared to a warm body. Turning away from the pillows, I'm now facing him.

The first night we stayed here, he faced me even though he was sleeping on the floor. Now, all I see is the blanket pulled up over his back. I can't tell if he's sleeping or not, but his breathing is even. Maybe I'm reading too much into this.

I know I'm not, though. Why else would he choose to sleep on the cold, hard floor? Slamming my eyes shut, I try to fall asleep, but it doesn't stop my mind from spinning.

"Is everyone ready to go?" I hear mom call out from the hallway.

Shit. I didn't realize I overslept. Now I can't remember if I set the alarm on my phone. If I did, I slept straight through it. I jump out of bed and change clothes as fast as I can. It takes me a few moments to realize I'm alone in the room.

Turning around, I don't see Tristan's makeshift bed on the floor. The extra blanket is neatly folded and placed on the dresser. The pillows he used are stacked beside the bed. There was no good morning kiss or anything from him. His bag is also gone.

How hard was I sleeping? Hopefully, he didn't decide he was done with me and leave with one of my siblings.

I shove my dirty clothes in my bag, grab my toothbrush and hurry to the bathroom. Luckily, it's not occupied. I've never been late getting up for anything. Rushing around trying to get all the things done in a short amount of time isn't fun, and I can't do things like this again.

My siblings are bustling around in the main area of the beach house. I can hear them bickering while they gather the last of their things. At least I'm not the only one out of sorts this morning. The only thing left to do is pack my toothbrush and fold the comforter. I'm not even going to worry about my hair. A messy bun will suffice for the ride home.

When I get back to the room, the comforter is gone, and my suitcase is sitting on the bed waiting for any last additions. Even frustrated with me, Tristan takes care of me. I do not deserve him in my life.

I tuck my toothbrush into the side pocket and glance around the room one last time. Everything is exactly how it was when we came in that first night. He really thinks of everything. I sip up my suitcase and roll it behind me as I close the door. Even if things don't work out between us, this trip will be my favorite one I've ever taken with my family.

tristan

THE DRIVE back to Asheville has been mostly silent. A few questions here and there, but Paula and I haven't touched on what happened last night…between her brother or us. This feeling is completely different than how it was when we drove to the beach. That was peaceful and companionable. This time, there's tension and uncertainty. It's heavy, and I don't like it.

I went into this weekend feeling optimistic and hopeful. Not even about being her potential real boyfriend, but in growing the friendship we had started after we agreed to this arrangement.

Now, I don't know what to think, or feel, after last night's confrontation. I thought she might bring it up when we stopped to get gas, but she only asked if I wanted anything while she ran inside to go to the restroom.

It's just hard because my heart is tied into this now. I

don't want to lose her, but I also can't stand idly by while she gets trampled on by her big brother.

"Do you want me to stop and get anything to eat before we get to your house?" Maybe opening up some dialogue will help.

She doesn't say anything for a moment, and I worry she's fallen asleep. Her head is leaning against the window, and her eyes are closed. She's been in that position for most of the four hour journey. I wish I knew what she was thinking.

"No, thank you. I'm pretty sure I have food at the house."

"Oh, okay. I just wanted to be helpful."

"You have been Tristan. More than you know." Then she doesn't say another word.

I don't know how I'm supposed to read into that. Even though I'm the type of guy that can roll with the circumstances in most occasions, I can't do that when it comes to relationships.

Right now, I don't know if I pushed her too far when I told her she needed to confront her brother while we were at the beach house. And now, I don't know that she ever will as defiant as she can be. She always tries to do the right thing, unless it's blackmailing me into going on this vacation with her. I smile remembering how that went down. Even though I was pretty mad at the time. It was clever.

We pull into her driveway and I put her car in park before turning it off. Opening the door, I hurry around to her side and open hers.

It's a lot colder here than it was down by the beach, and I'm already missing the temperature difference.

As soon as she's out of the car, I pop open the trunk and grab her suitcase and comforters.

"You don't have to carry them in for me." She doesn't sound annoyed. But she doesn't sound like she wants me to come inside either.

However, my mother would be horrified if I let her carry her own bags inside.

She takes out my duffel and sets it beside my car. I have a feeling today isn't going to end the way I expected it to do.

Not just on her part, but on mine as well. I need her to figure out what she really wants, and she needs to figure that out as well. Not because I want her too, though. She needs to want to do it.

Because, despite how much she doesn't want to work at the winery, I saw a little spark of interest at being a part of her family legacy. Which is fine by me. I can't tell her what to do with her life, and I want her to do whatever makes her happy. But I also know if she's not all in, she's going to end up resenting her family.

Following her to her door, I wait for her to unlock it and push it open.

"You can set those right there." She points to a spot just inside the door. "Most of that stuff is dirty clothes, and I need to wash comforter to make sure there isn't any sand in it, because my mom is right. That stuff gets everywhere and never goes away."

I do as she asks and set her stuff down in the front

entryway. Luckily, there's only one comforter she'll have to wash because the other one I packed away in her bag after we bought it.

I hate this weird feeling between us, and not knowing where I stand. The only reason I slept on the floor last night was to give her space, because she seemed like she needed it, and I didn't want to smother her. But maybe that was the wrong thing to do, because this morning, she's acting as if she doesn't want anything to do with me.

"Look," I say at the same time as she's set as she opens her mouth to speak. "You go first." I concede what I was going to say so she can say what's on her mind.

She clears her throat and shoves her hands into the pockets of her leggings. "Thank you for coming with me this weekend. It was a lot of fun."

"Yeah, I've never been one for beaches, But I had a good time."

"So, what you're saying is you'll be my fake boyfriend on anything I have to go to?" Her use of the word fake makes my stomach drop.

"Well, I mean, I kind of thought I was your actual boyfriend. But yes, I will go anywhere you ask me to."

"You know what I mean." She waves away my comment. "Anyway, I have a lot to do to prepare for the next week, so I'm gonna go do that."

"Oh, okay." What else can I say. It's a clear dismissal.

I reach in for a hug and give her a soft kiss on the cheek. "Look, I know things were weird last night, and a lot of stuff happened, but I'm going to give you your space so you can figure out what it is you want and what you want to do. Because even though I told you to live day by day and in the moment. And to take a shot on something new. I don't know if I can be in this back-and-forth space. You need to figure out what it is you want, and if I'm a part of that."

Her entire body stiffens, and I know without a doubt I've said the wrong thing. But it's too late to fix it now.

She pulls away, and that's the end of it. I flinch because I can't act like that one motion doesn't sting.

I don't know if it's the end of us, but it's the end of this conversation. I know she doesn't want to get into it right now, after last night. I think I've learned my lesson about pushing her when she is not ready to be pushed. I just learned the lessons too late.

"Okay. Well, I guess I will see you around."

She simply nods her head, and I back out of the doorway.

I guess this is what I get for wanting more when she wasn't sure she was ready for it. But I can be patient. It's all I can do, even though every cell in my body is telling me to go in there and apologize for acting like an ass.

"You look depressed," Dale leads us into the soon to be studio.

They've made a lot of progress since I was last in this space. There's still so much to do, but it will come with time.

"I'm fine." I sigh.

I'm not. It's been four days since the beach trip, and I haven't heard from Paula. I don't know what's happening, and it's driving me bonkers.

"No, you're not fine."

"How can you be so sure?"

"It's because I know that look and nothing good ever comes from it. I take it things didn't go well on the trip with the girl from the flower shop."

"How did you know that was where I went?"

I don't remember telling him that specific part. I don't even remember telling him I was going with Paula. So how did he find out?

"We may have played a gig at the bar over the weekend." He's no longer looking at me and studies every possible thing he can in the studio. "And Eric may have let it slip."

I swear to God, that man is nothing but a gossip. He might actually be worse than the moms of some of the kids I went to high school with. Hell, even my mom is a pretty big gossip, but she has nothing on the local bartender.

"Wait, you played a show? Who did you have help you with the equipment?" A tiny part of me is hurt I wasn't included. As much as these guys drive me up the wall, I love them and working with them. Paula was wrong, I do know what it's like because these guys are like my siblings. I spend more time with them than I do my own family.

"Calm down. It was an acoustic show and we set up ourselves. Now, what happened while you were gone?"

There's no hiding anything now. I might as well confess all the events that transpired.

"It was going great until it wasn't." I run a hand through my hair because this next part is entirely my fault. "I may have stepped into something I shouldn't have."

"What do you mean?"

"It's this whole thing with her siblings and the company they own. They want her to be a part of it, and she said she was going to tell them that she didn't want to do it. And I may have confronted her about it, when she told them she would think about it."

Now Dale is shaking his head. "Oh, Tristan. There's one thing you should definitely learn. Do not get between a person and their siblings. They may dislike them. They may fight and argue. But at the end of the day, they love each other and they will always stick up for each other."

"Is this coming from personal experience?"

I've only known Dale to be with one person since I've known him. I mean, of course, he has had other relationships. But I've only seen him in his current one. And he is head over heels happy with her.

"Let's just say, once upon a time, I tried to get between a girl and her family, and it did not work out well."

"Did you use any of the situation as song inspirations?"

"I plead the fifth. You know that shit can get me in trouble legally."

"Okay, okay, I'll stop asking for the gory details. But what did happen?"

"It was a whole thing." He sighs and sits on a makeshift chair of boards. "Her brother treated her like crap, and I stepped in, but I wasn't nice about it, and things went badly."

"What did you do, fight him?"

He doesn't answer me. Well, I guess that answers that question. I don't know why he thinks I would fight somebody. I am not that type of person. If anything, I'm usually the one breaking up arguments and almost fights with people we surround ourselves with.

"Well, nothing like that happened when we were there. I did get in his face once, but she doesn't know about that because he never brought it up."

Now I'm about to sound like a jerk. "But the last night where we were there, I did get an argument with her. That's where I feel like I overstepped. Now I haven't heard from her in days, and I feel like it might be the end of us."

"All you can do is give it time, man. I don't know what else to tell you?"

"Do you have any idea how incredibly hard that is for me?"

"Yeah, I know you're patient to a point. Not that I'm speaking from personal experience." He grins up at me.

"That's only because all of you wait until the last possible second to do anything, and it's mind boggling."

"You have to trust the process, and that's my process most of the time."

"I guess."

I don't tell them that a part of me wants to go talk to Pierce. I'm really debating whether or not I should. if anything, just to clear the air between us. I know he could feel my glare the night everything went down. But that would be another area where I'd be overstepping my boundaries, and I do not want that to get back to her.

"You hungry?"

Dale's question pulls me out of my thoughts.

"Yeah, I could eat."

"Well, let's get out of here. There's not much else we can do here today. And I'm starving."

"Let's go." I already know where we're going. It's a good thing because me and Eric need to have a little chat.

CHAPTER TWENTY-ONE

IT'S hard working in a flower shop when you don't feel like basking in all the lovey messages people want to add to their orders. Most of them I don't have to see. But there are a few customers who refuse to use the online ordering system, and I have to write out their messages on a notepad. These are the times I consider a different profession.

"Why are you so sad?" Emily asks from behind me and I knock my phone off the counter.

Reaching down to pick it up, I see the background. It's the picture my sister took of me and Tristan. It doesn't help my mood, but it does make me smile.

"I'm not sad," I stand up. "Just feeling a little blah."

She studies me for a moment. She starts with the hair piled on top of my head, to the oversized sweatshirt and then the leggings. This isn't my usual attire, but it's all I had the energy to put on. This past week has been brutal with trying to get my sleep schedule back, and sleeping alone in my bed. Damn Tristan for making me want him next to me at night.

"You can keep lying to yourself, but I know the look of heartbreak. Your outfit was basically my uniform when Alex dumped me in college."

"Nope. I'm perfectly fine." It's a lie. I've been a mess since Tristan dropped me off. But I'm not taking the full blame for that. He didn't say a single word the entire ride home. Then that little speech he gave before he left. The whole thing was weird.

"Alex was an idiot for dumping you back then."

Emily grabs one of the extra stools and slides it next to me. Oh, so she isn't going to drop this. Great. Other than Sam, I'm the least likely to show my feelings. Though, I guess she can tell something is up by the way I've come into work this week.

"Agreed, but he's made up for it." She pulls her sweater over her hands. "No offense, but you look like you need to talk."

"I really don't." In all actuality, I do need to talk to someone. These past few weeks Tristan has been my sounding board, but he hasn't bothered reaching out to me. There's no way I'm talking to my siblings about anything because two of them will give me so much shit, and the rest wouldn't understand.

"Well, I guess it's a good thing I'm caught up on orders. I can hang out up here with you all day."

There's no point in fighting her on this. She will do

what she says. At least until I open up. She always has to play mother hen to everyone. It's not a bad thing, it's who she is. It used to be my role in my family until I got tired of babying grown adults. Although, I never had to do that with Pierce. He's above all that if you ask anyone. Even when he did need help, I was too intimidated to do anything.

"What is it that you want to know?" Maybe if I open up a tiny bit, she won't pry too much.

"What happened on your trip? I mean you weren't exactly a ball of sunshine when you went, but you weren't this, either." She waves her hand toward me. "Did Tristan do something to upset you? Or, was it something with your family."

Damn. She hit the nail on the head. Sometimes I wonder if she's psychic. She always seems to know what people are going through without them saying anything. It's one of the many things that make her a great step-mom.

"Both?" I groan before placing my arms on the counter and burying my face in them.

"Can you elaborate?"

It would be so much easier to do this without facing her, but I know she won't be able to hear anything I say. Kai has the music up louder than normal which is irritating. But I'm pretty sure he's doing it to get under his sister's skin. The joys of having siblings. Lifting my head, I turn toward her.

"I should have never taken Tristan as my fake

boyfriend. Not when I started having feelings for him prior to going, and knowing he had feelings for me. Even though we became an actual couple while down there."

Her grin speaks volumes. "That's amazing." But when she sees my face, she back tracks. "Or, maybe it's not?"

"No, it is. But we both made some missteps, and now I don't know where we stand."

"Have you talked to him about it?" It's the obvious question, I know that. But it doesn't make it sting any less.

"Um, no?" I tighten my ponytail then take a sip of water to stall. "I don't like confrontation. He pretty much put the ball in my court. I'm so used to trying to please everyone, I don't know if that's the only reason I want to be with him, or if I need to figure out my own shit. I've never done this whole relationship thing."

"You should probably talk to him." She doesn't say anything for a few moments. "And how did things go with your family?"

"Shockingly, most of the time was fun. There were two instances with my big brother that weren't great. One led to an argument with Tristan. And here I am."

"Is he still pressuring you to work at Starlit Fields?"

"Yep. And I told him I'd think about it. Which isn't exactly true, and why Tristan was upset."

Emily scrunches her eyebrows together. "Why would that matter to him?"

"It was one of the conditions we had before we left.

He would go as my fake boyfriend if I told my family how I really felt about working at the winery." In the end I didn't fulfill my part of the bargain.

"I see." She taps her fingers on the counter. "Do you love him?"

"Pierce? Of course, I do. He's my brother."

She gives me a pointed stare. I know who she meant, but I don't know if I'm ready to cross that emotional bridge. Maybe if I wait her out, I won't have to answer.

The look is so much like the one my mom used to give me when I was teenager, I break within minutes. "Fine. I don't know if it's full-fledged love. But I do know I was, am, falling hard for him. The entire trip he always put me first. My well-being, my decisions, all of it."

She glances over at my phone and points to it. "I hate to break it to you, but that is far more than falling. You really need to talk to him and set things straight. Trust me, I know all about not talking about things. You don't want to go down that road and have regrets."

She's told me about what happened with her and Alex. It was all because of some bullshit her dad did, and he was a scared teenager. Actually, now that I think about it, him and Tristan are a lot alike. I've always been slightly envious of her relationship. Except when something similar happens with me, I push it away with everything I have. I'm so not normal.

"I'll talk to him. But, I may need some supplies before I do."

"Just name it." She slides off the stool, and turns for

the hallway. "I should probably go back to building orders."

"I thought you didn't have anything to do."

She shrugs her shoulders. "I had a feeling you needed my time more."

With that parting remark, she walks away. She really is a psychic. Now to figure out a way to talk to Tristan without getting defensive. That will be my biggest hurdle yet.

A truck that looks like my dad's is sitting in my driveway when I pull in. Once I put the car into park, I look out the window. Sure enough both my dad and brother are sitting in the front seats. Pierce is the first one to get out, and he opens my door for me.

Why is he being so nice all of a sudden? The only thing I can think of is my promise to think about working with the family. My stomach drops and I know I need to tell them I don't want to. At least, not the way he wants me to.

"Hey, Sister." He waits until I turn the car off before helping me out. This is weird behavior from him. What is he playing at?

"What are y'all doing here?" Once I'm out of the car, Dad gets out of the driver's seat. "I didn't get a text from you."

"We need to talk, and I had a feeling you wouldn't answer a call from me."

As bad as it is to say it, he's not wrong. I dodge calls from him like it's a sport.

"How did you know what time I get home from work?"

"Parker." I knew the answer before he said it. He's the only one who keeps track of my work schedule. He's also the only sibling who will drop in for surprise visits. This is out of character for both Pierce and our dad.

"Let me open the door really quick. I have a feeling this is more than a driveway conversation."

"It's definitely more than a driveway conversation." My brother nods and follows me down the sidewalk. Dad brings up the rear. I swear we probably look like a line of ducklings.

After unlocking the door, I push it open and walk inside. I set my bag by the door and continue to the living room. Whatever they want to talk about is probably something I should sit down for. They rarely come out of their way to pay me a visit. Especially not out of the blue.

"Do y'all want something to drink?" Mom would be proud of me being a somewhat decent hostess.

"No, we're good," Dad takes a seat next to me. Pierce sits across from us on the recliner, and gives dad a look as if he was in fact thirsty. Sorry big brother, Pops spoke for you.

"So, what is this about? Did I do something?" I hate how unsure I sound, like I'm a kid in the principal's office. It's this moment I realize why Tristan told me I should have handled this when we were all in the same spot. I'll have to have this conversation multiple times. While I have them here, I might as well tell them I'm not working for the winery.

"No, you didn't do anything wrong. But, we do have some things to discuss."

Oh shit. He's using his dad voice. I don't like that tone. No matter what he said, it always meant I was in some sort of trouble growing up.

"Well, we might as well get this started." I lean back until I feel the cushions on my back. Something needs to bring me some comfort since Tristan isn't here to provide it.

Pierce leans forward and places his elbows on his knees. Okay, so they both mean business. "I need you to be honest with me when I ask you this."

"Okay?" What the hell is he getting at? He said we need to talk, but this feels very ominous.

"Do you really want to work at the winery?"

That's not the question I was expecting, and it knocks me off kilter. My first instinct is to sit up and reassure him I do want to work with the family. But I take a second to think it through. Acting before thinking hasn't gotten me anywhere, and there's no way I can avoid this conversation. I have a feeling they won't leave until I give them an answer. Actually, I know they won't. It's why they came to my house instead of somewhere public. My escape would have been easy in any other situation. Here...not so much.

"Not in the way you want me to." I shrink into myself and wait for the chastising I'm about to receive.

"How would you like to be involved?" Pierce asks. He hasn't changed his sitting position. It's how he signals he's listening, but he's also in business mode.

"I'm not sure yet. But ideally, I think there are ways you can partner with Whoopsie Daisy."

Dad turns toward me, and I sit up because I don't want him to be disappointed in me. "Do you love the work you do at the flower shop?"

It's a question he's never asked me, and I'm shocked he's showing interest now.

"Yes. I'm learning a ton of new things. Once I have arrangements down, they plan on me helping with some of the brides and special events. I love the people I work with, and I like creating with my hands."

He must see the spark of joy in my eyes as I talk about the shop because the smile that overtakes his face is something I haven't seen in a long time. At least, not when it comes to me in relation with Starlit Fields.

"I know you wanted all of us to take over the winery, but my heart isn't in it. It never has been."

Dad pulls me into a hug. "I'm so sorry if I ever made it felt like you didn't have another choice. I only ever wanted to make sure you knew this company is available to you. Forcing you into something you hate was never my intention."

"You didn't force me." I pull away from him. "It's the whole reason I moved out and found different jobs. I needed to find what I wanted. The only reason I said I'd think about it is because I didn't want to let y'all down."

"That's my fault," Pierce moves from the recliner to

the floor in front of me. "I shouldn't have pushed you as much as I did. You probably don't remember, but when we were little, we used to talk about all the things we were going to do when the winery was ours. Then you pulled away. I thought working together would bring us closer to each other."

"Dumbass." The word is out of my mouth before I know it. "Sorry, Dad. That's the reason I stopped coming around. I thought you hated me when were teenagers. But it makes sense. That's when I realized the winery wasn't what I wanted."

"I'm sure you've called me worse."

I don't agree or disagree with him. "How did you realize I didn't really want to take on a job?"

This time he scoots back. Is he scared I'm going to lash out?

"I may, or may not, have heard you and Tristan arguing at the beach house. You know you didn't have to bring a fake boyfriend to deal with me. Though, things sure seemed real between you. Especially after he got in my face that first day."

"He did what?" This is the first I'm hearing of this.

"It was after you stormed out of the house. Don't be mad at him. It was well deserved." He glances around the house. "Where is he anyway? I figured you two would be inseparable once we got back."

"Um, I may have been kind of bitchy toward him. We said some things, and he said I need to figure things out."

"Have you?"

"Yes." I realized it after talking with Emily. This relationship stuff is hard and terrifying, but I need to stop hiding when things get difficult. He was right about leaving us in limbo. All it's done is make me miserable. Not knowing how to handle things between us has cost me more sleep than I'd like to admit. "I'll need your help, though."

tristan

WHY IS this equipment so freaking heavy? It's not like it can even go in the studio yet. Dale ordered it while I was with Paula and didn't think about the delivery date. Now we have to store it in the house. I guess it's a good thing he hasn't moved in.

"Just pile it all up in the living room." He grunts while helping the delivery guy carry in the sound board.

"You realize we'll have to move all this again when the studio is actually ready, right?" This is one of those things I was talking to him about the other day. He does whatever pops into his brain without thinking through the logistics.

"Yes, I know." He grunts as they set it against the wall. "And don't start, I already know you're going to tell me I should have waited for you. But, we're going to hire someone to move it to the studio. I'm getting too old for this shit."

"You said it." I laugh and put down whatever is

inside this big box. "Oh, will you need me this afternoon?"

"Not that I know of. This was the big thing on the agenda today. We might get together later tonight to put down some dates for the next tour."

"When will that be happening?" He said we were going to chill for a while. I would prefer they wait until all this construction is done and they have started on a new album before they make plans. But I'm not their manager. They do like my input, so I definitely need to be there for that.

"I don't know. Which is why we're meeting." His smile is smug. "Why? Do you have a hot date with the flower shop girl?"

"Her name is Paula. And, no." I don't mention I still haven't heard from her. Eric said she's been in the bar, but it was only to grab food. She didn't stay. He didn't provide any other details. I have a feeling he knows more than he's putting on.

At this point, I'm ready to reach out to her. I lay down in the middle of the floor and stare at the ceiling. I haven't gotten any sleep since the vacation and regret everything I said to her. If I'd known it was going to be like this, I would have kept my mouth shut.

"What do you need to do?" He moves to stand over me. "And why are you lying on the floor staring into the void?"

"I've got an appointment to see an apartment. And I'm contemplating a nap." If sleep wouldn't elude me, I wouldn't have this problem. But I know I won't be able to do that until I've talked to Paula. This is what I get for putting the onus on her to decide what she wants. I know what I want...her.

"Do you hate us?" Dale asks and pulls me out of my maudlin thoughts.

"Why the hell would you ask that?"

"Because you're looking for another place. You've never said anything."

Good gravy. I sit up and shake my head. "No, but I need my own space. No offense, but bringing a date back to a house full of people isn't exactly romantic."

He busts out laughing. "I'm just giving you a hard time. I hope the apartment is everything you need it to be."

"Thanks." My phone dings in my pocket. My heart rate jumps. Is this it? Is she finally reaching out?

"Are you going to see who it's from?" He nods toward my pants. "It could be life changing."

He's right. It could be...for better or worse. I'm almost scared to see who it's from. There's no time like the present, I guess.

I pull out my phone. The first thing I see is the picture from the botanical gardens on my lock screen. I would give anything to go back to that moment. We were tucked away in our own little world. Nothing could touch us.

When I check the message notification, my stomach drops.

"That's not a good look. I guess it's not Paula."

"No, I'm pretty sure it's her brother." I open the

message to read the entire thing, and dread fills every part of me.

UNKNOWN NUMBER

Tristan, it's Pierce. We need to talk.

My thumb hovers over the phone to respond. He probably wants to warn me away from his sister, and I don't know if I'm ready to hear that. But I have a question first.

TRISTAN

How did you get my number?

I take a moment to save his contact information in my phone. That could be useful later.

PIERCE

Parker gave it to me.

There's no way Parker would have willingly gave him my number. I mean, I don't know him very well, but it doesn't make sense why he would. Now I'm curious.

TRISTAN

Oh. What day do you have in mind?

PIERCE

Tonight if possible.

This raises my hackles. Why the rush? I mean he's more expedient than his sister, sure. But from what I gathered during the trip, he's not exactly team Tristan.

Sure. Send me an address and time.

That sounds very threatening, and I consider editing the message. In the end, I leave it as stands. A few moments later an address and time shows up on my screen.

"Sorry, Dale. I'm not making the meeting tonight. I have other plans."

He nods and helps me off the floor. "Remember, no fighting. I'll bail you out of jail if I have to, but I'd really rather not. We've built a positive reputation here."

"We all know I'm a lover, not a fighter." At least, I am for now. Who knows what will happen tonight. Either way, I plan on giving Pierce a piece of my mind.

It's dark when I pull up to the address Pierce sent me. I'm pretty sure I saw a sign for Starlit Fields when I turned into the driveway. Why in the world would he have me meet him here? Surely, he won't act like an ass on company property. I have no idea what's in store for me, but I don't see anything good coming from this. His actions have proven he's not my biggest fan.

The number of times I pulled out my phone to call Paula today is unreal. At one point Dale took my phone away. I wanted to tell her Pierce contacted me. Dale told me it would be better if I go to this meeting and see what her brother has to say. Honestly, I think he's doing his best to protect me from heartbreak. It's a part of life, though. He can't protect me from things I willingly seek out. I'll go through hell on earth for Paula, even if this meeting doesn't go well.

A truck is sitting outside what looks like a brick house. Maybe he lives on the property. I guess I'm about to find out. I put my car in park and tuck my phone into my pocket before stepping out. Deep breath in. I count to three and let it out. It's now or never.

The door opens before I have a chance to knock. Creepy. Was he watching out the window to see when I'd get here?

"Tristan, I'm glad you could make it. Please, come in."

His tone is unsettling. He's not as gruff as he was on the trip. Maybe I should be worried. Dale offered to cancel the meeting and come with me, but I told him it was unnecessary. Now, I'm not so sure.

"Um, thanks." I step inside and glance around. I'm pretty sure this used to be someone's house. It looks like it's been renovated to work as a business. What I assume is the living room has a basic set up, but there's no TV. A couple of couches face each other and there's a glass table between them.

The entire space is open aside from a room in the back. The door is closed, and I can only assume it's the office. Pierce leads me to the couches and motions for me take a seat. He sits on the couch on the other side of the table.

"I bet you're wondering why you're here." He leans back, completely at ease.

The best thing I can do is mimic his actions. Maybe he won't be able to tell how nervous I actually am.

"I am."

"I wanted to apologize for my behavior on vacation. I shouldn't have acted like that when we had a guest."

"Well, you shouldn't act like that at all. It's kind of an asshole move."

He laughs. What the fuck? I just insulted him, and he laughs it off.

"It was, and I'm sorry."

"That apology should go to your sister. You push her and make her feel like shit unless she bends to your will. I may not be close to my brother, but I know that's not how it should be between siblings."

He winces. Finally, a tiny fracture in his facade. "You're right. But since you brought up Paula, do you love her?"

"I don't see why that's any of your business." He really thinks everyone should answer to him.

"Humor me, please." He leans forward, awaiting my response. I'm not sure why, but I have a feeling my answer this holds importance.

"Yes." I don't elaborate. The when and why is something for Paula's ears alone. Her brother doesn't get to be a part of that.

"That's all I needed to know." He stands, and when I follow suit, he holds his hand out for me to stay. "Can you wait here?"

"Sure." Weird. That's what this whole thing is. I feel like I'm in a reality TV show, and the shoe is about to drop. Should I be concerned? Probably, but I'm invested and want to see what all this song and dance leads to.

Sitting and waiting is boring. I'm not sure how much time has passed, but I'm getting antsy. I stand and move to one of the floor to ceiling windows. It's pitch black outside. There are a few solar lights marking a path that leads around the house. The location of the winery is perfect. On a clear night you can see the stars twinkling. Maybe that's where they got the name Starlit Fields. It's fitting.

I feel hands move in front of my eyes. "Keep your eyes closed."

Paula walks me backwards, and based on the direction she's taking, we're heading back to the couch. Once she has me seated, she moves away. "Don't open them yet."

"Okay." My voice is barely above a whisper. I don't want to do anything to scare her away. To ruin this moment. In almost a week, it's the first time I've heard her voice.

There are sounds coming from directly in front of me. I can't tell what's going on. As much as I want to peek, I don't.

"You can open them." Paula is sitting on the edge of

the table. A bouquet of flowers in a vase and the photo I have as a lock screen sticking up in the middle.

"What's this?"

"An apology." She holds the vase out to me. "This is the first arrangement I've created on my own."

"They are beautiful." I set them on the table beside her. "But you don't need to apologize. If anyone does, it's me. I overstepped when I should have let you handle it on your own. You know your family better than I do."

"Shockingly enough, I don't. Pierce and I had a long talk. We cleared a few things up, and I will be working with the winery."

Damn she gave in. That's not what I want to hear.

She sees my face fall, and moves to sit beside me. "I didn't sell out to please my brother. I do want to be involved in the winery, but in my own way."

"How are you going to do that?"

"Well, this property is massive. With a few spaces added to it, it would be a great place to hold larger scale events. Like weddings. I happen to work in an industry where I could suggest it. As soon as everything is done, they are going to join forces with Whoopsie Daisy and the local wedding planner."

"Th-that is amazing." I pull her closer to me. "You get the best of both worlds."

"My thoughts exactly."

"I'm sorry for the way I acted the last time we saw each other." I take a deep breath, and keep going. "I really should learn to keep my mouth shut sometimes.

It's just that I love you, and the last thing I want to see is you hurting, or taken advantage of."

"You love me?" Her eyes are wide, and she's acting as if this is the most unbelievable thing she's heard. I guess Pierce didn't tell her about our brief interaction.

"I know we haven't known each other long, but yes, I do love you. I fell head over heels for you the first night we met, and with every interaction we've had since. You're it for me."

"This is completely out of my comfort zone. But I know in my soul, I love you." She throws her arms around me and smashes her lips into mine. I pull her into my lap for easier access. This is the next moment that will live rent free in my mind for days to come.

Applause catches our attention and I pull away. Her entire family is standing in the entryway.

"Were they in on this entire thing?"

"As if they would let me do this without them. You know how nosey they are."

Parker heads toward us until Pierce pulls him back. He almost runs into the wall with the force. Maybe Pierce isn't so bad after all.

Paula leans her head on my chest. How she has the ability to ignore their presence is beyond me. But the noise fades away and finally it's the me and the woman I love. There's nowhere else I'd rather be. Nosey family and all.

epilogue

IT'S sixty degrees outside and I'm sweating. The work that goes into events is more than I imagined. No wonder the rest of the group goes out for drinks after they wrap up. Is it too early to take a shot?

"Paula, you need to calm down." Tristan places his hands on my shoulders. "You don't have anything to worry about."

"Seriously?" I look around at the absolute chaos inside the venue my family built on Starlit Fields. "Nothing is where it's supposed to be. I don't think I can do this."

He moves one hand to my jaw, turning my face until our eyes meet. "Take a deep breath."

"Now's not the ti—"

"Take a deep breath." He cuts me off. This time it's a demand, not a request.

I do as he says. I breathe in until my lungs are full.

His focus is on me the entire time. He doesn't blink, only watches what I'm doing. "Now, let it out."

As always, Tristan grounds me whenever I start to spiral. "Thank you."

"You have me, the rest of the Whoopsie Daisy crew, and your family here to help you." I start to turn, but he brings my attention back to him. "We are not going to let your first event be anything but amazing. Samantha is making a list and handing out tasks. The only thing you need to do is finish putting the arrangements together and get them on the tables."

"But the DJ isn't here, and I can't get ahold of him."

"Let me worry about that. If push comes to shove, I can get on stage and perform one of the few scenes I did in high school."

"Absolutely not." I laugh. "No offense, but I've seen you act. It's no wonder you were part of the stage crew."

"Well, that's mean." He's holding in his laughter so I know he's not upset. He must think I'm calmer, because he pulls his hands away from me. I miss the contact already. "But I will track down the DJ. There will be music present for this party."

"Thank you."

Mom is walking toward us with a glass of wine in her hand. As soon as she reaches me, she hands it over. "I figured you might need this."

"You are a life saver." I take a big gulp. At least she doesn't think it's too early for booze. I hand it back to her, and she finishes it off. "Tell me everything is going to be okay."

Tristan tilts his head to the side. "I literally just told you that."

Mom pats him on the back. "Sweetie, sometimes it needs to be heard from a parent." Then she focuses on me. "I'm so proud of everything you have accomplished. This party will be the event of the season."

"Thanks, Mom."

She gives me a quick hug. "I'm going to make sure your brothers are doing their part."

"See, we have faith in you. This is your first event, and you should be so fucking proud of the way it's come together. I know working for both places has been hectic. But I've got you."

He reaches for my hand, and I let him take it. I fully expect him to take me somewhere to calm down, but he doesn't. He leads me toward a table that has the rest of the arrangements. "Let's get these babies done. Are there certain tables they need to go on?"

"Nope. The only one that has something different is the one for the family."

"Perfect, I'll start placing these while you work on the last couple of centerpieces."

He uses my hand as leverage to me toward him. Dipping me back, he kisses me long and hard. Whistles and clapping fill the space around us. Our friends and family are ridiculous, but at least they are supportive. Being honest about my feelings with them is the only reason I'm able to put on this event today.

I hold onto him like the life line he is. Finally, he lifts

me up and pulls away. "That was a bit of good luck. You'll get more when this shindig is over. I love you."

"I love you, too, weirdo." As calm and reserved as he is most of the time, he does like to make a spectacle of himself. He'll do anything to make sure I always have a smile on my face.

I watch him as he takes off, a vase in each hand. How did I get so lucky to find someone like him? It almost feels like fate had a hand in bringing us together. I glance down at the phone that started it all. I'm cherishing every moment I can with this man.

It takes a village to write a book. I would be nowhere without mine.

Wee One, thank you for making sure I'm writing when I'm supposed to be. Also, would it be possible for you to not watch my favorite shows in the same room? K. Thanks.

My bestie, Nessa, thank you for being my sounding board and supporting me all these years. I wouldn't want to do life without you by my side.

Stephanie, Alex, and Ashley...you have been my biggest cheerleaders while finishing this book. I don't think I could have done it without you!

Hubs, I swear one day I won't disappear for days on end when I'm on deadline. I'm building a process, I promise.

Boy Child and Grand, thanks for the untimely, but much needed distractions.

To my Patrons, thank you for your unwavering support! You have no idea how much it means to me! So, thank you, Donna, Crystal & Steph!

Readers, you truly make all this possible! Thank you for reading about the characters I create. Without you,

I'd be driving my husband bananas with all the stories I have swirling around in my head. So, I think he might thank you, too.

Do you want to meet more of the characters in Asheville? You can check out my books here. Or, scan the QR code to find out what some of the other residents of this small town are up to.

about the author

Katrina Marie lives in the Dallas area with her husband, two children, grand baby, and fur baby. She is a lover of all things geeky and nerdy. When she's not writing you can find her at her daughter's sporting events, playing with the grand, or curled up reading a book.

You can find Katrina Marie online in the following places:

Sign up for my newsletter: https://www.subscribepage.com/KatrinaMarieNewsletter

Website: katrinamarieauthor.com

facebook.com/katrinamarieauthor

instagram.com/katrinamarieauthor

bookbub.com/profile/katrina-marie

pinterest.com/katrinamarieauthor

tiktok.com/@katrinamarieauthor

patreon.com/katrinamarie